PRAISE

"Sublime in the purest sense of the word, Craig Gidney's gorgeous stories evoke beauty, terror, and wonder, often — usually — on the same page. He uses words the way a master artist employs paint, creating lush, hallucinatory worlds as beautiful as they are treacherous. A beautiful, heartfelt collection."
— Elizabeth Hand, author of *Generation Loss* and *Hokuloa Road*

"*The Nectar of Nightmares* is a haunting collection of stories, filled with retellings and reimaginings, transgressive versions of familiar tales from our youth. It's important work that's being done here, visceral and unsettling, paired with humor and hope. This is an author to keep an eye on, for sure."
— Richard Thomas, author of *Spontaneous Human Combustion*

"*The Nectar of Nightmares* is an incredible and breathtaking achievement. There's a sublime magic in these stories as well as a lingering danger, one that lurks at the edges of every page, waiting to draw you nearer. No one else out there is writing weird and wondrous fiction like Craig Laurance Gidney. Prepare to be dazzled and bewitched."
— Gwendolyn Kiste, Bram Stoker Award-winning author of *The Rust Maidens* and *Reluctant Immortals*

Also by Craig Laurance Gidney

Sea, Swallow Me & Other Stories
Bereft
Skin Deep Magic: Short Fiction
A Spectral Hue

the Nectar of Nightmares

This book is published by Underland Press, which is part of Firebird Creative, LLC (Clackamas, OR).

I though to give him a gift . . .

Edited by Darin Bradley
Book Design and Layout by Firebird Creative
Cover art elements by deryart / stock.adobe.com

This Underland Press trade edition has an ISBN of 978-1-63023-063-0.

Underland Press
www.underlandpress.com

the Nectar of Nightmares

stories by

Craig Laurance Gidney

CONTENTS

To the Memory of Eric Mueller
You are missed
Rest in peace

Beneath the Briar Patch

The war between Fox and Rabbit ended with a man made of tar and a briar patch.

Both of them just loved jokes. Real showboaters, that pair. Two centers of attention. Life of the party, times two. They were mostly good at making themselves laugh, rather than other people. Audiences were collateral damage. But what they liked even more was being the Best at something. If Fox made a funny face, Rabbit made an even funnier one. If Rabbit learned how to interpret a song with a series of burps, then Fox learned how to make his farts sound musical. If one could juggle three balls, the other would try to juggle six knives. On and on, it went, each trying to outdo the other. Oh, they wrote the book on competitiveness. Think Cain and Abel. Jacob and Esau. In that vein.

But one of them took it too far. It was inevitable. It's always funny until someone loses an eye. It was Fox who did it, but it just as easily could have been Rabbit.

See, Fox got it in that pea-brain of his to make a fool out of Rabbit because:

1. Rabbit had done something to piss him off (even Fox had forgotten exactly what that was);

2. Rabbit always gave good reactions (he was the Patron Saint of Butt-Hurt);

3. Because Fox was an asshole.

So Fox went down to the swamp, where a pool of hot black tar bubbled. He mixed the tar with a crude figure he made of sticks and bones he'd dug up from graves. He put raggedy clothes on the figure that he'd stolen from laundry lines. He gave the tar-thing glass eyes stolen from a little girl's doll, a maggoty potato for a nose, and a slice of watermelon for lips. A gator's over-ripe heart, bound with wire was placed in the thing's gloppy chest. Fox knew some Hoodoo, so he put the whammy on the thing and *Presto! Blammo!* It lurched behind him, a man-sized poppet.

Everyone hung out at the Briar Patch. It was kind of a speakeasy. You hung around and shot the shit with your pals on nights when Sister Moon wore her silver dress that made her look round and the sky was full of stars. The thorns of the briar patch were as sharp as nails, but fireflies swarmed in the branches and lit it up like a cotillon ballroom. Everyone was there: Bear, Dog, Cat, Hog, Hoot-Owl, and Magpie. They drank corn liquor that burned their throats and made them look cross-eyed. They all flirted, fought, and gossiped by the Patch. Of course, Rabbit was there. He was always there, laughing too loudly. Fox hid on the other side of the patch, and sent the tar-poppet into the crowd.

"Well, hello there," said Sister Goose. She waggled one of her false eyelashes at the dashingly dark figure.

The poppet said nothing.

"Wanna wet your whistle?" said Hoot-Owl, and the poppet wordlessly lurched away.

In fact, the Tar Poppet said nothing to anyone. He just lumbered along silently, just as Fox wanted him to. And, just as Fox predicted, everyone thought the poppet was rude and sullen.

Rabbit was the center of attention, in a cluster of folk including Badger, the Hen Triplets, Bear, and Dog. Presently, Hoot-Owl joined them.

"What's up with that uppity so-and-so over there?" he said to the group. "I gave him salutations, all gentleman-like, and that fool just up and ignored me. Why come to the Patch if you ain't gonna be sociable?"

Everyone's eyes drifted over to the shambling figure, who had apparently affronted Madame Buzzard, who was being consoled by Sister Goose.

Madame Buzzard was a drama queen for sure, but still; enough was enough. No-one owned the Briar Patch, per se, but Rabbit was, in an unofficial manner, its proprietor. It was Rabbit who arranged the shipment of moonshine, and he also spread word about the gatherings hither and yon. So Rabbit felt a certain responsibility for the Patch, and, just as Fox had hoped, Rabbit left his clique, and approached the poppet, who was now slumping by the bushes that surrounded the glimmering patch.

"Say there, sirrah," said Rabbit, "I hear that you're causing quite a stir in here."

What do you think the poppet, who now hid in a snare of shadow, said?

This incensed the eminently insensible Rabbit. "What's wrong? Sister Cat got your tongue?"

". . ."

"What's wrong? Can't you speak?"

". . ."

"Just nod if you can understand me!"

". . ."

"Do something! Wave your hand! Stomp your feet. Anything!"

". . ."

Now hidden in the bushes, Fox laughed silently at this. This was gonna be good!

If Rabbit hadn't been such a hothead, he would have noticed how the poppet's posture was poor, or the weird, sulfurous stench it exuded. But by now, Rabbit's head was hot enough to fry an egg on.

"Didn't your mama train you right? Are you crazy?"

To which he received an infuriating, ". . ." as an answer.

If he had been an engine, steam would have been pouring out of his ears and nostrils. He went into the shadows, and you know what happened. First a slap across the thing's face, then another, both of them sticking to the things skin. Then one swift kick, followed by another. By this time, Fox revealed himself from behind the bush, gasping with laughter until tears came to his eyes. Everyone at the Briar Patch gathered around and gradually figured out that this was one more battle in the endless prank war. Some of them joined Fox in laughing at Rabbit's misfortune, but a sizable group just rolled their eyes in disgust and moved away from the scene.

"You got me," Rabbit said. He sighed. "Now, have your boy here let me go."

Fox wiped a tear from the corner of his eye, and said, "OK." He made the appropriate movements and said the words of power to end the spell. And nothing happened.

Rabbit struggled some more. "Hurry up. I gotta pee."

Fox tried again, taking his time to avoid making a mistake. Hoodoo demands precision. But it didn't work the second time.

"What the hell," said Fox. He wasn't laughing anymore.

"Ha ha," said Rabbit. "Very funny. Let me go. Now."

"I'm trying, dammit. I'm trying."

Fox performed the spell, enunciating each word carefully, modulating his voice to its loudest pitch. He did all of the gestures in slo-mo. And still, nothing.

"I'm getting irritated, Fox."

"I don't know why it's not working. Let me try something else. Can you reach into all that tar? In there, you will find a gator's heart—"

"Ow!" said Rabbit. "It stung me!"

"Careful there. I bound it with wire . . . Now if you can just pull it out . . ."

Rabbit was—awkwardly—attempting this operation when something mighty strange happened. The tar poppet began to absorb Rabbit at an accelerated rate, until he was swallowed whole, from ear tip to hind leg. The poppet got fat, grotesquely pregnant with Rabbit's body. Madame Buzzard screamed. Sister Goose fainted. Fox cursed, horrified. Then, Rabbit's face appeared in the middle of its belly. "Help me," he croaked. And the poppet jumped right into the Briar Patch, taking Rabbit with it.

It was Sister Magpie who took control of the situation. No-one noticed her arrival. She appeared and vanished like a thief in the night. She was a sneaky one, with a penchant for snagging shiny little things. But she had a streak of wisdom, as bright as the white feathers that fringed her dark face. It was she who helped Goose after her fainting spell, and she who quieted the crowd.

"Brother Fox," she said when the hush had settled, "just what, exactly, did you do?"

Fox hemmed and hawed.

"Out with it!"

"Well, ma'am. Sister. See, I thought I'd play a little trick on Brother Rabbit. You see, last week he—"

"We all know about your tomfoolery. We ain't interested in hearing a bunch of Who-Shot-John stories. Just what was that thing that took our brother into the Briar Patch?"

Fox reluctantly told them about the poppet, how he had made it, and how he had lost control. "I don't know what happened."

Hoot-Owl had been silent until this moment. He swiveled his head toward the Briar Patch, then back to Fox, who had his head in his hands. "Hoodoo calls to hoodoo," he said. "Them that practice it, that follow it's ways always know when hoodoo is done. Hoo! They smell it, they taste it. In the air. Most hoodoo is small work. Tending to an ill one, fixing a broken heart. But big spells. Hoo! Big spells always get noticed. And sometimes, them that notice mischief like to have a little mischief themselves. Hoo!"

Maybe it was the corn liquor, or the shadows, but Hoot-Owls lambent eyes seemed darker. And the shape of his head more devilish, and tufts of his head feathers looked like horns.

He whispered (and the Animal Folk gathered closer): "I think the Conqueror caught him a whiff of Brother Fox's hoodoo witchery, and took the poppet to see what was stinking up the Patch."

A gasp rose like woodsmoke from the crowd. Madame Buzzard fainted this time, falling on the woozy Sister Goose. Buzzard was not a small creature.

Fox, and the surrounding Folk, were stunned to silence.

That name, and face it conjured. The Conqueror. All of them knew of him, the stories and campfire tales. No-one had seen him, ever. But all knew where he lived. Where he reigned.

And who was the Conqueror? Here are some of the various conjectures, rumors, tall tales and theories, in no particular order:

1. He was the worst kind of animal: a man. He was the sorcerer-king of some long-dead kingdom who was banished to the Briar Patch, where he ruled a fiefdom full of demons, witches, and various undead creatures;

2. He was no man at all. He was a living plant growing from the poisoned earth underneath the Briar Patch where he radiated his evil influence over all who came in contact with him;

3. He was neither man, animal, or vegetable. Rather, he was an evil spirit trapped beneath the Briar Patch by some eldritch spell that could end at any moment.

"I hear he eats souls," said Brother Bear.

"He eats bodies *and* souls," said Sister Weasel. "He cooks 'em up in a stew. Okra, onions, your blood as broth, and you as the meat."

"I've heard worse," said Hoot Owl. "The Conqueror is a god from some black region beyond space and time as we know it. A place with many fanged and tentacled monsters."

Fox squeaked, "What's a tentacle?"

Sister Magpie said, "Enough of this . . . speculation. We all know what must be done. We have to go beneath the Briar Patch, and rescue Brother Rabbit. Who will join me?"

No-one stepped forward. They looked at the ground, or sipped moonshine, or preened their feathers or their fur.

"No-one?" she said, glancing at the cowering crowd. "Then it's just you and me, Fox."

"Hold up," he said.

"Don't even," she said, marching towards the tangle of thorns. "You were the one who started this. You need to make this right."

Fox followed her, tail between his legs.

There was no way to avoid the thorns. They did their best, but in the end, their entrance into the Conqueror's realm was clearly marked by the tufts of fur and clumps of feathers left on branches. You can bet that there was much cursing. When they finally got to a clearing, they rested, nursing the scratches and scrapes they'd sustained.

"Damn!" said Fox, "I hope we can find another way to get outta here. I don't think my hide can take any more abuse."

"Shh!" said Magpie. "We ain't the only folks here."

Both fell silent, listening. Above them, Sister Moon was in her full glory, wearing a gown that had just the slightest tinge of blue. Her fullness was caught by the snares in the branches, and the light she cast slashed into blue-white ribbons. Branches creaked, even though there was no wind. The two Animal Folk stood back-to-back, peering into the latticed gloom. They saw movement in the branches, shiverings and quiverings. And they saw eyes. Eyes of yellow and eyes of green. Red eyes, like dots of blood, and blue eyes, circles of sky. Eyes with centers like black stones and eyes with barbed thorns in their center. Eyes that looked at them with malice and mischief, curiosity and hunger.

"Let's walk," Magpie whispered.

"What direction?"

"Hell if I know."

Fox sniffed the air. Did he catch just the faintest whiff of tar? Or was he just imagining it? Did it matter, considering the current circumstances?

"Come on," he said, chasing the scent. Sister Magpie followed.

They walked in silence. It was tough going and required some measure of concentration. The briar branches grew wildly, in all directions. Some were low-hanging and had to be ducked under, and others had to be stepped over. Gingerly, to avoid further cuts. As they walked, the smell of tar became stronger. The night was hot and humid, and the two decided to rest before carrying on.

Fox said, "Do you think he's dead?"

Magpie stayed silent.

Fox said, "I never meant for this to go this far. It was just a joke. It was just a game."

Magpie cocked her head to the side. "Shh," she said. "I think I can hear something."

Fox heard it, too. Something moving on the dirt ground and over the branches. Something that slithered. It emerged from a particularly dense crosshatching, unravelling from some aperture like a rope made of green mint with patches of black soil. The snake was immense, with eyes the reddish green color of a rhubarb. It could easily swallow Sister Magpie whole, and wrap itself around Brother Fox and crush his rib cage.

"Greetings," it said in a voice that covered its syllables like moss over muddy stones. "Welcome to my father's realm." The voice was androgynous and mellifluous. It promised slow death, and bones hung beneath the Briar Patch, like ornaments.

Both Animal Folk stepped closer together.

Sister Magpie, pressed against Fox's fiery fur, said, "And where is your father? Might we have an audience with him?"

The snake's forked tongue flickered in and out of its mouth, tasting their fear. It said, "Why would you need an audience with him? I do not recommend it. He is not . . . *agreeable*, most of the time."

This time Fox spoke, perhaps encouraged by Magpie's boldness. "We have some business with him. Did you happen to see a man made of tar pass this way?"

The snake stayed quiet, as if considering the question. "I may have," it said.

"Which direction did it go?" said Magpie.

"Why," said the snake, sidling up to the pair, "would I tell you?" His green-red eyes flashed.

"Because," said Sister Magpie, "if you *don't* tell me, I will take your eyes. My, how they shine. You know how I like sparkly things, don't you?"

The snake paused. The reptilian face was unreadable, alien. But maybe—just maybe—it gave her words some consideration.

"Forgive my insolence," said the snake. "We get so few visitors down here, we have forgotten our manners." The snake crossed the dusty path. Both Fox and Magpie watched its progress carefully. The serpent's length was seemingly unending, inch after inch of mint-green and soil-black scales. It took its time. When its head reached the other side of the tangle, it turned toward the pair and said, "You were going in the right direction. That hoodoo thing was headed to the Conqueror. You are either very brave—or very foolish. Devouring you would have been a mercy."

Sister Magpie ruffled her black-and-white raiment in fury. She fluttered off the ground and darted toward the snake's brightly evil eyes. The snake hissed and dove into the brush quickly.

When they were sure the snake was gone, both of them collapsed in a heap of trembling.

"You were magnificent, Sister," said Fox, after they had regained some measure of fortitude.

"I don't know if I can do that again," she said. "Let's go on. I would like to be out of here as soon as possible."

They headed to the center, where the Conqueror lived. They did not talk about what would greet them once they arrived. There was no need. They said that John the Conqueror made the Devil himself scared. Haints turned even whiter than they were, after meeting him. Beautiful witches turned into decrepit crones after dealing with him. Fox and Magpie knew that any deal they made with the Conqueror could go wrong, horribly wrong. He did not abide by the laws of man, or of the Animal folk.

"How are you gonna convince him to let Rabbit go," Sister Magpie said, maybe to fill the silent gloom that had descended beneath the Briar Patch.

"I reckon I'll be straightforward," replied Fox. They had settled into an easy pace. He loped on all fours, and she flew when the way was clear. "I'll say, "Mr. Conqueror, I hope I didn't bother you with my little hoodoo spell. I promise not to work any mojo again. But, if you wouldn't mind, please let Rabbit go. It weren't no fault of his that he's here. He just got caught up in my foolishness.'"

"That sounds mighty nice, Brother Fox. It just might work."

"Or, it could fail horribly."

The voice came out of nowhere, and everywhere. It sounded like a screech. It scraped against the eardrums. Fox stopped dead in his tracks, and Magpie landed on the red fur of his back. The air in front of them thickened into blurred pearls of moisture until a shape the color of Sister Moon in her finest white gown hovered in front of the pair. The shape was formless and cloud-like. It had two almost symmetrical globes of reddish-green that suggested eyes.

"Who are you?" said Fox. His hackles were raised.

"That is entirely the wrong question," said the cloud-like being. *"The correct question is, 'Who was I?'"*

"All right then. Answer that question."

"My name was Sapphira, and I was cursed with great beauty. My skin was dark brown and glowed with health. I had amber eyes, and pleasing shape. I was also a slave and worked many long, hot hours picking cotton in unforgiving sun. My great beauty caught the eye of an overseer. He was an ugly, cruel man, with skin the pink color of a pig, and he had a pig's jowls as well. I would see him leering at me as I bent down to fill my sack. I knew what he wanted. And I knew my fate, were I to deny him."

The cloud-like being poured an image into their minds of a brown-skinned beauty with a muscular frame crowned with a glory of thick plaits.

She continued: *"I prayed to the Lord and to the Savior nightly to protect me from his advances. One night, my cabin-mate, who was much older than I, laughed at my prayers. She called them pitiful. 'That white bearded man and his blue-eyed son ain't gonna save you, chile. Only one thing can.' And she told me about the Conqueror, and how to reach him. I did as she instructed, making the offerings of blood, saying the right words.*

"He took me to his lair, in the middle of the Briar Patch. Oh, he is fearsome to look at, as you will soon find. I told him my troubles. 'What will you give me, if I help you?' he asked. 'What will you take?' I said. He told me that my soul was his for five score years. That seemed a fair bargain. Oh, if only I had known! He lent me some of his power.

It poured into me, into every inch of my being. It set every fiber of my being on fire. I was baptized with mojo."

When she returned to land above, the haint continued, she found herself imbued with wisdom. She knew which plants could heal, and which could kill. She could ease pain with a touch, and got premonitions. She also knew how to communicate with the Animal Folk. When the overseer came around and made his bid (in an unnecessarily lewd manner), she spoke a Word of power to his horse. The horse followed her command, and threw the overseer. The overseer suffered a couple of broken ribs. He never bothered her, or any other female slave, again.

Armed with new power, she became arrogant and careless. She became known around the plantation as the resident witch. Fellow slaves approached her for love potions, ailments, and, occasionally, revenge. Knowledge of her power spread, until even poor white laborers asked for a spell or a tonic. When word of her witchery reached her owners, the punishment was swift and brutal. She found herself facing a lynch mob armed with rifles. Not even her newfound powers could save her from a crowd eager to see her demise.

"I been down here nigh on twenty years. Longer than I was alive."

She seemed to have concluded her tragic tale. Brother Fox said, after a moment, "Sounds like a run of bad luck. Surely, *he* didn't cause you to die. Did he?"

The rhubarb eyes flared. *"Not directly. But he could have warned me, you know."*

"Fair enough." said Fox, "We will heed your warning."

"Sister Sapphira," said Magpie, "did you happen to see a poppet made of tar pass by."

"I did. It was a terrible sight to behold. It seemed to have something trapped in its gooey belly, something that hollered and hooted. I reckoned it was a victim for one of the Conqueror's devilish plans. It went that way." The phantom extended a cloud tendril in the direction of a tunnel of thorns. *"I would not go that way, if I were you."*

After that pronouncement, the spirit winked out, like a snuffed candle. Magpie and Fox looked at the tunnel of thorns for a full minute. It was dense and dark, and the thorns in there looked sharper than the other thorns. The worst thing, however, was that at the tunnel's end, they could see a light. An ominous reddish-greenish glow.

Brother Fox said, "If we survive this, Brother Rabbit will owe me, big."

Sister Magpie said, "True, that." She hopped up on Fox's back and settled down.

They started down the tunnel, silently. They didn't speak. It seemed out of place here. Besides, they had to concentrate on the path before them, which was narrow. The ground was full of fallen thorns. Fox had to navigate carefully around them. It was chilly in the tunnel, though it was high summer outside of the Briar Patch. Magpie shivered on Fox's back, and both Animal Folk's breath misted out from their mouths, beaks, and nostrils. Gradually, the shining red-green end of the tunnel got larger and larger, until they reached the end. They emerged from the tunnel, and saw:

1. A nightmarish clearing filled with bloody green light that glowed from nowhere; the light was in the air itself, saturating it and coloring everything in the circular clearing;

2. Brother Rabbit lying unconscious in the remains of the tar poppet. He held the gator's heart in his arms, as if it were a baby. A puddle of tar spread out from his body. At first, they couldn't tell if he was alive or not:

3. And the worst thing of all: the Conqueror himself. He grew out of the ground, mingling human and vegetable parts randomly. His legs and torso were naked bone enrobed in thick vines. Two stalks extended from the torso—evidently, his arms. His face was human enough, with a wide nose and thick, sculptural lips. He stood at least several hands tall, like a scarecrow. On every part of his body bloomed morning glories in an array of colors. This last bit was the most disturbing, for it made clear that the Conqueror was not a natural thing. He was something Other and unknowable.

It was Fox who broke the silence: "Is he dead?"

The face of the Conqueror swiveled, took the measure of the two Animal Folk. The voice of the Conqueror did not come from the finely shaped lips. It came from the throats of the blossoms. You could see them vibrate with the effort. It was not one voice, but a chorus of them.

Collectively, the Conqueror said, "Which one of you dared to make the creature of tar?" The sound rasped over feather and fur.

Fox stepped forward. The ghastly face of the Conqueror imprisoned him in his stare. The rhubarb light came from his terrible eyes.

"Why did you do this thing?" the voices said.

Fox glanced to Rabbit, and saw that he was breathing. He licked his muzzle, and spoke: "Oh, Great and Honored one. I apologize for using witchery for my own petty mischief. I am sorry to have vexed you so."

The vegetable man said nothing. The morning glory blossoms quivered like lips.

"Go on," whispered Sister Magpie, "tell him *why* you made the tar poppet?"

"Oh, Great One, the reason I performed such hoodoo was to trick Brother Rabbit. There was no other reason. See, Brother Rabbit is much better at tricking me. I thought that I would do him one better. Sir. Your Grace. Your Honor." Fox glanced down at the earth.

A sound arose from the Conqueror. A rustling, as if a wild wind had crept into the clearing. It was underscored with a booming sound that shook the very Briar Patch, causing the thorns and branches to clash together. Fox looked up to see the face of the Conqueror laughing. It was a roots-deep sound, and his flower-mouths laughed along with him.

It stopped as abruptly as it started.

"You are foolish," said the voices, "but, I admire your treachery. Your love and hate for your friend and enemy must be strong. Still. Do not dare to use Power again. I will know. And I will not be pleased."

Fox and Magpie shivered at the harshness of the voices. The face of the Conqueror relaxed, his eyes closing. At once, the bloody green light faded, and—

They were out of the briar patch. The sun was just beginning to rise.

"What," said Fox.

"Just," said Mapgie.

"Happened," said Rabbit. He was now awake, blinking the sleepiness out of his eyes.

Fox was so happy, he could have kissed him. But he did not.

"We saved your hide," said Sister Magpie, after they regained their composure.

"After *he* almost killed me," said Rabbit.

"Don't facing the Conqueror count for anything?" said Fox.

Sister Magpie began preening herself, plucking out the various thorns and twigs that had caught in her feathers. "You two, stop. Now's as good a time as any to call a truce."

Both Fox and Rabbit looked at each other abashedly.

"Come on, now. After all we went through, I'm not gonna leave until you two make up."

Brother Fox and Brother Rabbit agreed to end the prank war. They both swore on their mama's graves; Sister Magpie made them before she flew off into the dawn.

Did they keep their bargain? That's another tale, for another time.

Myth and Moor

I've lost my way.

Emily heard the small voice beneath the rustle of the morning winds. It was a child's voice, high as a piccolo, full of distress.

I've lost my way.

She turned in her bed, faced the bedroom window. It was still dark outside though the horizon was bleeding at the edge. She was in her dressing gown and her hair was coiled up in a braid beneath her bonnet. The floor was chill beneath her bare feet, but Emily didn't bother to put on slippers.

She saw him at the window, beneath a shrub. A young boy in tattered dull clothing. He had blond hair beneath a cap and the chubby cheeks of a cherub. His skin was as thin as tracing paper. She could see things beneath its surface. Moth wings, curled ferns, as if he were a stuffed doll. And his eyes were a pale turquoise blue that glowed.

The moor was full of ghosts. She had seen them many times during her long walks, men and women and children with translucent skin, earth-colored clothes and bewildered expressions. They wandered the windy grasslands, drifting here and there like scattered dandelion fluff. They never seemed to see her, appearing to be preoccupied by some private matters. Emily ignored them and for the most part, they ignored her. A couple of times, one of them might follow her for a brief spell or tried to get her attention. Eventually they would dissolve like mist. The ghosts moved their mouths, but no sound issued forth.

This young boy was the only one who she could hear. That must have meant something.

"Who are you?" Emily asked.

The child reached through the fogged glass and touched her hand. The fingers on her flesh felt like icicles made of feathers. They tickled her; gooseflesh rose in response.

I've lost my way.

The refrain echoed in her brain. She knew that voice, that angelic boy soprano that resounded throughout the church nave. Then, she recalled the face.

"Heath Linton," Emily said.

He'd gone missing a little over a year ago. Vanished. Had he been kidnapped? Beset by highwaymen? Or fallen down some hidden hole on the moor, in pain and in the dark? Heath was like Emily; in that he loved the countryside. She'd even gone on a few walks with him.

Why was he there, outside of her window? And why could she *hear* him?

Emily's late mother could hear the spirits of the departed.

"I hear my babies in the wind," she told Emily on her deathbed. "They're saying 'We've come home, Mama! Let us in!'" Her mother was referring to her two sisters, taken from them by consumption. Just like her mother had been, in a cruel twist of fate.

Papa and Charlotte and the attending physician had believed that Mama was in the throes of delirium and that the phantoms she saw were induced by the fever that raged in her frail body. Emily knew otherwise. Because she could see them. Her sisters, pale and faintly luminescent in their calico pinafores were standing outside the window, waiting patiently for their Mama to join them.

Emily didn't tell anyone that she could see the dead, Not even Anne, her closest sibling, nor Bran, even though he adored dark stories. Now, she could hear them. Or, at least, Heath.

He faded as the sun rose over the moor, melting into dew. Soon he was a cutout made of green grass and purple heather.

Isobel Linton, Heath's mother, dropped by the parsonage that afternoon. She was a husk of the woman she had been before her child went missing. Her vitality had been robbed by grief and a reliance on laudanum. She had never been a beauty; her face was too sharp and angular, her body stout. But she did love fashionable dresses in bright, gay colors. Now everything she wore was black as coal. Her brown hair was messily hidden beneath her bonnet, and she emitted a rank odor, as if she had given up on hygiene.

"I would like to see your father," she said, slurring her words ever so slightly.

"I'm afraid that he's visiting Jane Berkshire. She asked him to prayer over her husband Innocent. He's in a bad way."

Mrs. Linton's eyes were widely dilated as she stood in the foyer, and Emily thought she saw her wavering.

"I have no idea when he'll return," Emily said. She knew that she should invite the woman in, offer her some tea. She wanted to comfort the woman, and tell her that she'd seen Heath this morning. But she knew that Mrs. Linton was in a fragile state, that she should keep her abilities to herself. Besides, there was an erratic air about the woman. Madness radiated off her person.

"I'll tell Papa that you stopped by."

"Will you now," Mrs. Linton said. "Which one are you? Charlotte, or Anne? I get you mixed up."

Emily said her name.

"Oh yes. The wild one. The one who prowls the moor with a huge black dog like some fey thing. Some folk say that you're peculiar. Wandering the wilderness with no escort." Mrs. Linton narrowed her eyes.

"I like to take the air," Emily said. "What of it?"

Isobel Linton eyed her suspiciously. "You must know that things live out there. Unnatural things. Wicked creatures. Heath never learned that. He just blithely went hither and yon."

Her brother Bran entered the house, interrupting this odd conversation. His bright orange hair was in disarray, as usual. He paused, sensing the tension in the air. This sudden appearance seemed to calm Isobel Linton, her wild eyes losing their focus.

"I should be off," Mrs. Linton said. Then she grasped Emily's arm in a vicelike grip. "The land is beautiful, but it is also treacherous. Please be careful. I would not want you to suffer the same fate as my little lamb."

"What was she on about," Branwell asked Emily after Isobel Linton left.

"I think she believes that someone—some thing—is responsible for Heath's disappearance."

"Some *thing*?" Branwell replied. "Such as what? A boggart or hobgoblin? Jenny Greenteeth? Or maybe Black Shuck came and carried the child off in his jaws."

"Bran!" Emily said and batted at him. "It is tragic, to lose one's own child. I won't have you laugh at her misfortune."

Branwell sucked his teeth. "It is tragic, I agree. She is addle-brained due to grief. But she has four other children and a husband that she must stay steadfast for. Her idle speculation won't see their needs met."

"Maybe not," Emily said. "'There before the grace of God, go I.'"

Heath appeared to Emily during the next few days. Sometimes in the morning, sometimes at dusk. Always when she was alone or with Keeper, her tall mastiff. He always said the same thing, over and over. A litany or a plea. Maybe that was all he could say. He was trapped in some nether land between life and death. Emily assumed that he would go to Heaven. Surely, the Lord would want such a pure, innocent soul as that little boy.

For a week, Emily ignored the revenant. Her talent for seeing the dead was a secret she closely guarded. Papa, being a man of the cloth, frowned upon superstition, considering them coarse and sinister. But she and her siblings loved the supernatural and the uncanny. The four of them dreamed up worlds full of romance and dark intrigue, and all of them wrote poetry and stories filled with magical occurrences. But this was not a fairy story or a gothic novel.

There was some reason that Heath manifested, some message he wanted to impart to her.

I've lost my way. I've lost my way.

One Wednesday morning, before the sun rose, Emily took Keeper and her walking stick and stood outside, waiting for the boy's spirit to materialize. She waited in the chilly, damp meadow while Keeper sniffed the ground. In the dim light, he could have been the demon hound of the moors. He was an imposing dog, and many people were frightened of him.

She heard Heath before she saw him. His plaintive chant sounded in her brain, drowning out the chorus of early morning birds. Then he formed. First, a floating face. Then hands and torso. The rest of him, the legs and feet, were invisible. His spirit was faded and unfinished, just the impression of a child of six.

He said his piece.

She replied, speaking aloud to the shimmering boy: "What do you want to tell me? How can I help you?"

He melted into mist. Then, maybe a yard away, his face reappeared. A face made of moss, bracken and heather with milky blue eyes.

. . . *my way* . . . The words echoed in Emily's brain.

She followed him out onto the moors.

The sky was grey and white, much like Keeper's coat.

Keeper bounded ahead of her, flushing out an ornery grouse, which took to the air with reluctance. The mastiff expressed his excitement with barking and a kind of canine acrobatics, standing on his hind legs. Emily laughed, then whistled for him to follow her.

The day was chilly, and the grass still wet from the morning dew. Her older sister would certainly chastise her. She could hear Charlotte now: "You'll catch your death out there. Consumption or the 'flu." Maybe so, but there was a small part of her that believed that she was invincible. That she was part fairy, an elemental changeling burdened with a human form. Papa would frown on such supernatural whimsies and sternly remind her that the Christian soul had no room for competition with nonsense.

At first, Emily thought Heath was leading her to the Linton farm. They raised a meager flock of goats and sold milk and cheese. But they breezed right past the farm. Emily shivered, thinking about the ominous behavior of Isobel Linton. *The land is beautiful, but treacherous* . . . Heath led her deeper and deeper into the moors, past fields embroidered with newly emerged flowers. Sometimes, he was fully materialized, a boy of seven, gamboling in the fields like a lamb. Other times, he was a wan impression, thin as tracing paper. They skirted the edges of farms, past pens full of sheep and chicken coops.

This is madness, Emily thought to herself. Emily knew she had a reputation as an odd duck, and that Papa's parishioners thought she was queer and unladylike strolling through the heather and gorse unaccompanied, but she didn't care. The wide-open grasslands, clad in green, yellow, and purple, were sacred to Emily, holier than the cold stone and hard pews of the church. Here, where she could have been the only person for miles, was where the Lord's awesome powers of creation were on display. God lived in the wild, and not in the staid, ritualized confines of Man's civilization. It was here, in Nature's church, that she felt like herself. Not the little sister, or the vicar's daughter, or the household chatelaine. Here, in the sea of grass, she was a poetess. Words and images drifted to the top of her head. The fluttering moths, the darting mice, the slinking lizards all demanded to be captured somehow. Ballads, odes, and couplets danced around her head during these solitary constitutionals. Chasing the ghost of a child was exhilarating.

A few hours later, Emily found herself in a relatively sparse area, a place where the grasslands gave way to coarse, shrubby vegetation, and bizarre large rocks exploded from the land. They were mottled grey and brown outcroppings that seemed to have materialized out of nowhere. They belonged in a land of volcanoes, not in the English countryside. She could easily imagine some ancient monstrous lizard walking around there. Heath's outline had faded to a mere disturbance in the air, his voice silent in her mind.

A single, stunted tree burst out of the ground. It was a tough, wizened-looking thing, with grasping spindly branches, nude of any leaf. There was something about the outline of the tree that reminded her of a human figure frozen in time. The branches grasped at the air. She saw that the branches were hung with tiny, bizarre ornaments. Spiky little things strung up with wire that rattled in the wind, making a strange percussive sound.

Then she saw the severed leg. A haunch of some animal, probably a goat, lay in front of an opening in one of the rocks. The black-and-white hair of the leg was matted with blood and seething with flies. The top of the leg was gnawed on, with strips of glistening red raw meat surrounding a yellowish bone.

It looked out of place in that barren space. Nature's cruelty in a naked display. Emily loved all the creatures of God's creation, and her first emotion was one of horrified sorrow. She could almost feel the terror and pain of the hoofed creature as it was rent by—by what? Wolves were unheard of in this part of the country. Wolves were creatures of the forest, not the wide-open grasslands. Maybe one of them had wandered there. Could it have been a bear? Whatever had killed the poor goat had done so with much violence, and furthermore, had devoured the rest of the animal.

She saw some movement near the dismembered leg—

"Keeper!" She called. He had been nosing near the carnage. He perked up his ears. Then, he laid flat on the stony ground, his ears laid back, and bared his fangs. She heard him snarl at someone— something that lurked in that crevice. Fear chilled her as she ran towards her beloved mastiff. He was formidable, but no match against the ravening creature that hid within that slice of darkness. Emily ignored the hampering of her muslin dress as she moved from grass to stone.

When she reached his taut, alert body, she smelled the stench of rotting flesh. It was so nauseating, the smell, that she was dizzy. The smell was layered, the foul and sweet mingled together, and so overpowering that she began to gag. But the smell did not just come from the severed limb. It came from within the crevice. That mouth-like opening. It was the perfume of Hell, gaseous and putrefying. Death himself would be taken aback.

Then she felt the tingle of being seen by something unseen. Eyes were in the dark. Feral eyes, measuring her and Keeper, considering the meat they would provide. The thing that ate the goat could easily dispatch her.

Then she heard something stir in the shallow cave. A rasp of some rough fabric, like burlap, against stone floors. She recognized that sound; after all, she was a genius at needlework and knew all of the qualities of various fabrics. That's when Emily knew that whatever lived in that depression was human.

Keeper growled, low and guttural. Emily gripped her walking stick so tightly that her knuckles became as white as snow. A sudden gust of wind came off the moors, bending seed heads and blossoms. And something moved in the dark. Emily knew that she should run. She took far too many risks, and laughed off her siblings' concerns about stray highwaymen or gypsies looking to do harm to her person. Now, their hectoring concern came back to her, tenfold. Fey girls could get their throats slashed. And Keeper, as ferocious as he looked, was daft and was just as likely to abandon her as he was to protect her.

A cowled figure, garbed in a dun-colored monk's robe, emerged from the crevice. Emily immediately saw that the person was grotesquely thin. The hands that emerged from the voluminous sleeves had long fingers, longer than was natural, and the nails were untrimmed and sharp. They reminded Emily of the bare switches of some shrub. The person had to bend in order to leave the overhanging rock, and unfolded itself with insect-like maneuvers to its full height. The elongation of the limbs suggested some illness that caused deformity. A sliver of Christian charity underscored the tumult of fear wreaking havoc in her mind.

"The meat is mine! It is not thine!" the cowled figure said. The voice was high and reedy. "I have killed the beast and alone I shall feast. Away with thee!"

"Gentle sir, I meant no offense," Emily said. She was intensely aware of the space between them, and the heft of her walking stick. Her long skirt would impede a hasty retreat. "I will be on my way."

The figure observed her for a moment, then threw back the hood of the cowl. At first, Emily couldn't make sense of the face that was revealed.

The skin was blue, the color of the woad dye that ancient Celts used in battle. The blue was not just on the face, it was also on the neck. A mane of hair, white as flour, erupted from the scalp, some of it braided and haphazardly entwined with objects, such as the skull of a field mouse or a bird. The sharp features suggested that this was a female figure, and now that she thought that, Emily could perceive a womanly shape beneath that rough cloth. The slight protrusion of breasts, the curved hips. It was the sharp glitter of the nails that caught her eye. They were more like claws. And they were iron in shade. Tiny knives, embedded in wizened hands.

This was no human thing. It—she—the dweller in the rocks—was some nightmare creature, belched forth by the bowels of Hell. Emily lifted her skirts, and began running. Then she stopped.

Isobel Linton's drug-addled warning surfaced in Emily's brain. *Keeper! Where was he?*

Emily spun around, scanning the grasses. Then she saw that her beloved mastiff was at the feet of the blue-skinned hag. Her iron-like nails hovered above his snout. She found herself heading back to the rocky plateau.

"If you harm him, you fiend, I shall—" she gasped out.

The blue hag calmly glanced in Emily's direction. Her iron claws clacked together over the dog's head. Keeper, fool that he was, sat on his haunches and stupidly wagged his tail.

"No harm shall come to the hound," the hag said. "I have no quarrel with him."

"Good day, madam," Emily said. "We will leave you to your . . . repast, and trouble you no further."

"I have no particular quarrel with you either, sylph. The rest of your kind, alas! They call me hag, witch. Black Agnes, Black Annis. Never 'madam.' All I want is a bed of earth to lay down, a bit of meat for my pot."

"Miss Agnes, is it?" Emily said. "I cannot apologize on behalf of my brethren. We can be a rude people, nasty to those whose looks and beliefs lay outside of Christendom. Once, in Brussels, I saw a group of men say horrible things to people whose only difference was that their skin was dark."

"Skin as dark as mine?" The blue woman seemed to be amused at the thought.

"No," Emily replied. "Even darker than yours! And with hair of wool that they can craft into elaborate sculptures."

"How curious," the hag said, and bent to stroke the underside of Keeper's jowls with her metallic fingers. He closed his eyes in pleasure while Agnes muttered, "You're a sweet one, aren't you?"

A gust of wind seemed to whirl up from nowhere. It chilled Emily to the bone, even though she wore a bonnet and had a shawl wrapped around her shoulders. She glanced up into the sky, saw grey and white clouds creeping across, obscuring the wild blue sky and the yellow sun. They were as thick as clotted cream.

"I really should be going," Emily said.

Black Agnes stopped stroking the dog, casting a glance up at the sky.

"You'll be caught in the rain," she said.

"Not if I hurry," Emily said. "Here, Keeper!"

"It'll be a wild one, that storm will," said the blue woman. "It will wash the likes of you away. Trust me, child. I have lived in this wilderness for many an aeon."

"Yes, Miss Agnes," Emily said, trying to quash the note of anxiety that crept into her voice. Keeper looked up to her, his deep brown eyes wide with concern. No doubt, he could sense her unease.

"You are afraid of me, child." Black Agnes stated this as a fact. "As I said before, I have no quarrel with you or your hound." She flashed Emily a gummy smile. It reminded Emily of dolmen pillars sprouting from black earth.

Nature conspired against Emily with a squall of air followed by the icy pinpricks of rain.

"Come, and be warm around my fire," Black Agnes said. "The rain shan't last too long." The blue-faced, iron-clawed figure beckoned from the opening.

Emily knew that she should leave this ominous place and walk to the parsonage through the driving rain. She'd done so many, many times. She would be in front of the fire in two hours, three at most, and Anne or Charlotte could warm her up with a cup of tea. That would be the sensible thing to do. She thought of Heath Linton. Surely, he had led her here for some reason. There was no doubt that this blue monstrosity was responsible for his disappearance.

But she wasn't just the minister's daughter. There was another, less proper Emily in her heart. An Emily that loved adventure, a young woman enthralled with the macabre and the numinous. That Emily wanted—even *needed*—to follow this eldritch figure into the Stygian darkness. And it was this feral part of her nature that led her and her dog to follow the hag beneath the earth.

Agnes had gathered the bloody shank of meat and stood in the rocky lobby of the cave when Emily and the dog entered. The rain came down in full force. The sky turned crow-black, and the moorlands became a sodden swirl of purple heather, yellow gorse, green grass, and brown mud. The storm was violent and stunning, the Lord displaying his awesome power. A crack of lightning, purple-white, razored the air.

"It's a wutherin' deluge," Black Agnes said. Emily turned to see the woman with the haunch of bloody meat in her glittering claws. Drops of blood flew in the wind, landing on stones and in her hair and on the rough-spun robe she wore. The woman didn't care that she was being baptized with liquid offal.

"Come on, then," the witch said and continued walking. Emily paused, both exhilarated and terrified in equal measure. She was leaving the above-world, full of light, family, civilization, and Christian doctrine for a sojourn in a lightless, lawless place.

What wonders will I see here, she thought. *What terrors?*

She turned from the dripping curtain at the cave's mouth to follow Black Agnes. Keeper followed at her heels.

It wasn't hard to follow Agnes. While it was dim, Agnes cast a kind of soft lambent light. Her blue skin illuminated the rock walls, bounced off of molds and lichen that clung to the stones. The ground beneath their feet sloped ever so slightly.

"Agnes," Emily said after a few minutes of walking, "how long have you lived here?"

Agnes paused, as if considering the question. Then she strode on through the darkness.

"The measure of time is a concern of mortals," she finally said. "Many days, many nights. Before you, or your grandmother were born. Before your kind set up stone buildings to live in, before your kind tamed the earth and the animals that roamed it."

"Do you have parents? Sisters? Brothers?"

"No," she replied harshly. "I have always been the same. No birth. No death. I just am. Things like me don't have families. I assume you have one. A family."

Emily stayed silent, because it seemed that the witch-woman was peeved. They passed down one path, turned into another. The air here was cool, and a damp, musky smell rose from the dirt floor. There were no animals underground. No insects, bats, or lizards. No badgers or voles. Maybe Agnes had eaten them all.

"I do have a family," Emily said, if only to fill the awkward silence. "My mother died when I was young. Papa never remarried. I have two sisters and a brother. There were two other sisters, but they both died of consumption."

She thought of them now. She and her siblings had created imaginary countries full of intrigue and romance. She could hardly wait to tell Anne and Bran about her encounter with Agnes. Outright sorcery wasn't a part of the Gondal canon, but since Anne had a taste for the gothic, Agnes would surely enflame her imagination. And Bran could paint a magnificent portrait of the blue-skinned witch. As they walked through chambers, Emily forgot her fear momentarily. Her excitement at this adventure drowned it out. It was as if she had been suddenly transported into *The Castle of Otranto* or one of Lord Byron's more fanciful poems.

So taken away with these fanciful thoughts, she dawdled a little behind Agnes. For a moment, the glowing blue figure was a mere dot. That's when the chill returned.

There's no way the caves beneath the moors are this extensive, she thought. The close ceiling of the crevice opening had expanded until the ceiling was as high as any cathedral's. The parsonage could fit in this chamber. In fact, the entire population of Haworth could fit inside. Glancing up, she saw stalactites dripping down from the ceiling like monstrous candles. There was a world beneath the windy grasslands. A hollow earth, a deep place where things like Agnes lived. She thought of the fairy mounds in the stories her late mother told her, of how their architecture did not obey the laws of nature. Those things were full of endless hallways and confusing mazes.

She and Keeper rushed to catch up with Black Agnes. Emily heard her shoes and Keeper's claws echo throughout the large cavern.

Down and down, deeper and deeper they went. Where were they going? Papa spoke of how Hell and Satan existed in the mundane world. Hell wasn't pitchforks and wicked women carrying chalices of their excrement. It was idle gossip, rivalry, and unkind thoughts. Agnes clearly was from a strange outskirt of Hell. Supernatural, pagan, and somewhat feral rather than outright malevolent. Did the blue woman have a soul? Could she be saved? She seemed to have emerged from some Pre-Christian period, when the ancient Celts spilled blood in honor of warlike deities.

Eventually, though, Agnes stopped walking, having come to a dwelling place of some kind. One wall of the cave was covered in rough jagged crystals, clear stones with a violet-tinge. The floor was worn smooth by a thousand years of foot traffic. Emily saw a bed of sorts, a pallet of cowhide and straw. A stone "desk" sat in the center of the crystal room, made of boulders with flattened surfaces. Agnes flung the dripping haunch on the top. She spoke a word that made Emily think of the howling winter wind out on the moors as it combed through frosted vegetation. It was a lonely sound, redolent of death and endless fields of white. And out of the whiteness, there was a spark.

And then there was light in the cave. No visible fire or particular source; it was as if the shadows had been shredded. Emily saw the crude furniture—a couple of chairs made of what looked like petrified wood, and a shelf against a bare stone wall, filled with—

"Oh," said Emily. "Oh, how marvelous!"

There were sculptures on the shelf, maybe thirty or so. They were lacy and porous chimerical creatures, perhaps three apples high. Emily saw that they were made of bone—tiny mouse, bird and badger skulls perched atop things with bizarre anatomies—winged voles with spiny vertebrae, creeping cats that wore necklaces of bird skulls. The eye sockets were decorated with stones and crystals and the negative space between the bones were filled with dried flowers and entwined with bits of bracken. Emily prided herself on knowing the flora and fauna of her beloved moors. She saw rusty sheep's sorrel, white mouse ears, and yellow asphodel interlaced with fern leaves and rushes. It was such delicate and precise work, one that only could have been done with a poet's soul and a saint's patience.

"You like them, sylph?" croaked the blue hag with iron thorns on the end of her hand.

"Indeed, I do," Emily replied.

Black Agnes cackled, a surprisingly endearing sound. "Would you like to see them dance?" she asked, and flicked her wrist and whispered a word in the language of the moors.

The strange sculptures began to move. Not in disjointed ways, but with a silky, fluid grace. Winged things took to the air while lizards made of bone slid up and down the walls and the earthbound creatures slinked around the stone cave.

Keeper comically barked at the advancing bone fauna and cowered away.

"My mother and my father are the land itself," Black Agnes said between bites of the meat. Bits of gristle and sinew flew as she ate. "It reared me. Was my nursemaid and my teacher."

Emily felt kinship with this creature. Both were daughters and caretakers of a beautiful and often cruel landscape. Emily sat on one of the crude chairs, away from the witch and her gory mastication. How could something so brutish create something so beautiful?

One of the animated figures approached her. It had the legs of a deer, the wings of a jackdaw and the skull of a human child. Tiny moths fluttered throughout its stout ribcage.

It was undoubtedly a human skull. The head of a child of six or so. Agnes had decorated the eye sockets with milky blue chalcedony. They stared up at her, imploringly.

It was Heath Linton's skull. It all came back, the reason for her journey underground. Had Agnes enchanted her somehow, made her forget her quest? She remembered the boy's shade, filled in with the flora of the moors. It came flooding back. A child with the voice of an angel. That angelic voice floating about, hanging from the rafters. His small hands, held out for Keeper to sniff and lick. The games Emily and he would play, darting among shrubs, hiding behind the stones. His bright voice, calling her name. The time they waited out a sudden storm in the ruins of a barn, and the stories she told him to pass the time. The boy made of flowers and moths, that appeared outside of her window, the coolness of his ghostly grasp.

Was this Heath Linton's fate—to end up in the belly of a pagan witch and have his bones desecrated? Emily could sense him, his spirit, somewhere in this cave beneath the sea of grass. He filled her brain with images and sensations. The rending of his flesh by iron-clawed nails. The cracking of his bones, the roasting of his flesh. Emily could taste his meat, tender as veal, tough as venison. She heard the pop of gristle, the grit of bone. The taste of the organ meat, all liver-flavored, the metallic gush of blood.

I've lost my way, he'd told the ancient witch that, a year ago. Heath had been incapable of understanding evil. His young mind thought that Black Agnes was some kindly old woman, an eccentric lady who dyed her skin blue. The sheer terror he must have felt when she dragged him fathoms beneath the earth to feast upon his flesh.

Her infatuation with Black Agnes came to a sudden end.

I have to kill her, Emily thought. She knew that it was a rash decision. She didn't want to die in some demon's lair. But she couldn't allow such a horrible presence such as Black Agnes or Annis or whatever she called herself to live. She had to do it for poor Heath's honor. She thought about the pain and fear he must have felt.

A tide of rage washed through her body, as red as the blood of Christ that hung in Papa's church. She could take her walking stick and brandish it like a weapon. But a quick glance at the iron claws of the ancient witch, blue as a harebell, made the tide subside. Could Black Agnes even actually die? She had lived through the ages, so what use would a tussle with a 'sylph' like Emily have? Like the badgers, or pheasants, or the earth itself, Agnes was a product of the moors. Savagery had a place in the natural order of the world.

"You have been very kind to me," Emily said, standing. Her knuckles were white as she gripped the walking stick. "But I'm afraid that I must be off."

The witch held one of the bone creatures in her arm tenderly. She gave Emily a piercing stare. "You will forget me," she said. "For that is the way of things like myself. Your sojourn will be nothing more than a dream, if even that." There was a note of unbearable sadness in the blue woman's tone. "I see, in your eyes, your great love of this wilderness, sylph. No harm shall come to thee."

Emily was unsure of what to say to that. She wanted to embrace and to rend the crone in equal measure.

. . . A crack of thunder sounded, and she found herself at the mouth of a stony crevice in the earth, watching a storm. Keeper lay by her, resting at her feet. How long had she been here, watching the storm? It seemed that she couldn't recall. All was a blur of wet rain and grassy ground.

She waited until the last of the dark clouds blew over the sky and patches of sunlight broke through.

Before she ventured out into the soggy landscape, Emily felt something in her hand.

It was a child's skull with two milky blue stones placed in the eyeholes. The teeth were entwined with harebell blossoms.

For one brief moment, Heath Linton stood in front of her, whole and unmarred. He grinned at her, his baby teeth gleaming like pearls. Then he faded from the air, like an afterimage. Emily stared at the spot where he'd stood for a good while.

She glanced back into the cave.

Then she went on her way, eager to leave whatever slumbered there alone.

Fur and Gold

The Beast waits.

Sometimes, he hides in the House. The trappings of humanity spark memories, some of them pleasant. The kitchen, with its pot-bellied stove, reminds him of warmth, and food. The bedroom, with its massive canopy bed, makes him feel safe, somehow.

The House has fallen and rotted. Mold creeps along the walls, in black and green tones. The ceiling is webbed with cracks in the plaster. Dust is heavy as snowfall on the black stove. The carpets are fouled with droppings and urine.

The human within recognizes this. And when the human within is awake—this is when the Beast leaves the House, and thus, his humanity. Into the overgrown grounds, thick with bushes and thorns, full of the scent of night and his fellow animals. The Beast smothers the human within, with wildness and instinct.

One time, the Beast went to the second floor of the House. In one of the rooms, there was a mirror. The human within him woke, catching his reflection. Instead of skin and clothes, he beheld mangy, tangled fur, alien eyes, fangs, and a blunt snout. Horns protruding from his head. A lolling tongue.

The human within cried out, in fear, in horror. The cry was not a human cry. The Beast ran from the image, terrified. The Beast does not go the second floor anymore. The Mirror is evil.

The Beast waits, but does not know what he is waiting for. The waiting is instinctual, as inevitable and inexorable as the fur that covers his hide. Time has no meaning for the Beast. He just watches sunrise after sunrise, sunset after sunset. The moon rises, the moon sets. Sometimes, it rains, and others, it snows. Time, like the House and the Mirror, are human concerns.

Every now and then, the thing within the Beast's heart stirs. Certain sunsets can do that—when the sun descends in a fiery blaze of pink, orange, and red. Or when blue butterflies sip from the throats of the drooping white flowers. These feelings, so set apart from the Beast's perspective of sleep, hunt, fight, and flight are pleasurable. He allows the human within him to pause, and exult in the beauty.

One thing the Beast and human within both enjoy is the Rose. The Rose grows on a bush in the front of the house. It is the only bloom. It is a miraculous thing, this flower. The whorls of the petals are intricate and infinite. You could drown in them, fold upon fold of vegetable matter as soft as velvet. They hypnotize the Beast. The Rose changes color every day. It has been the red of arterial blood. Orange, like the rising sun. As cold and white as the moon. Sometimes, cerulean blue or metallic silver. One time, the Rose was transparent. Another time, it was reflective, like the evil Mirror. The Rose is never the same color twice. But in all of its hues, it glows softly. Lambent. Luminous.

To the Beast, the Rose has always been there. It, more than the House or the surrounding grounds, represents home to the Beast. Every day, he must visit the Rose, as much as a salmon must swim upstream. In rain, even in the cold heart of winter, the Rose grows and blooms. The human within the Beast recalls a story about the Rose. Scraps of story, that the Beast can barely understand, save as images. Something about the Rose not being of this world. The Rose belongs to some impossible place, to some impossible kind of being. Neither the human within or the Beast dwell on this point for too long. It is too disturbing.

He returns now from visiting the Rose, which then was the color of clover, fresh green. He slinks back into the overgrown garden behind the fence, and curls up for a nap. Later, when the moon is high, he will hunt the woods on his grounds and feast on small game. The Beast closes his eyes, and briefly dreams of the hunt, that dance of instinct, scent, and blood. Dream-rabbits and dream-pheasants flee before him. He gleefully rends their tender flesh. The satisfying crunch of bone beneath his fangs fuels his dreaming. Fur, muscle, and wings all dominate his mind. The hunt gives him great joy. During the hunt, the human within is totally submerged and dormant.

The Beast is a light sleeper, as most of animal-kind are. So when he smells a distinct odor, he is awake immediately. The scent comes in waves, and it is strong as it crests over him. A scent that he has smelled before, tantalizingly familiar. Auditory clues swiftly follow: the sound of hooves on the dirt of the lane. A word, and another float up in the dark pool of the Beast's brain, provided by the human within.

Horse.

Man.

A strange emotion overtakes him, something more complex than mere instinct. It is akin to what he felt when he saw the Mirror. The Beast cannot place the feeling. But the human within can.

Loneliness.

Annoyed, the Beast struggles with the human within. The Beast wishes that he could see the human, to kill it efficiently with a bite to the jugular. He wishes that the soul trapped in his body would die.

Instead, the Beast stills his body, refusing to let the soul inside of him react.

The man and the horse slowly approach the House. The Beast is torn. He wants the man to pass by. Very few humans pass by; those that do are full of the rank smell of fear. He also wants to destroy the man. (The horse is innocent.) Humanity enrages the Beast. He wants to kill the man, and punish the man that lives inside of him. Perhaps killing another human being will quiet the restless spirit within.

The horse clops down the path, dragging a wheeled contraption along with it. The Beast can tell that the horse is exhausted. It is an old animal, probably too tough and stringy to eat. The man is also tired. With a dark-adapted eye, the Beast can see through the bushes and grasses that the man can barely keep his head up. He will probably pass by. Besides, the man is as old as the horse; not much meat there.

But, the cart stops, right in front of the path leading to the House. Why? Does the man think to spend the night in there? The rage grows in the Beast's heart, hot as an ember. But the reason for the pause is even worse.

The human has begun to speak, that hideous habit of mankind. It is an unnatural method of communications, to divide and catalogue the world with noises. The man within him recognizes these sounds, these words. Unawares, the soul within him has gained the upper hand, through trickery and stealth.

"What a marvelous rose!" says the man, apparently to the mute horse. "My son would love it, don't you think, Madame?"

Madame, presumably the name of the nag, snorts at this, no doubt, responding to the address. The Beast observes the man through the latticework of the fence and the mesh of leaves. The old man snips the Rose with a pair of shearing scissors. The severance between the bloom and the bush is intense. It wounds him, Man and Beast both. The wounds inflicted by knives or bullets or teeth—surely, they could not hurt more than this. It is because of this pain, needle-sharp and piercing, that words burst from the muzzle of the Beast.

"Thief!"

The man shouts, startled. The nag whinnies with fear. She canters backwards, finally catching his animal stink. The Beast crouches in the thicket, yellow eyes focused on the old man.

The old fool dodders backwards, much like his Madame. He seems to find both his voice, and his footing. "I meant no harm, sir. It's just, your house appears to be abandoned. Please, accept my apologizes."

The words come quickly, violently, like a thunderclap. "I will not accept your apology. That Rose—it was the only thing I loved in this world. And you have murdered it. There is not another like it!" The anger crests, like a wave, and the words leave him. A sound overtakes them, a keening howl, a yawp of rage and loneliness that shatters against his eardrums. The Rose has changed its color in its death; it is now some nameless shade between the mauve of the gloaming and the amber-brown of a fawn. The shriek terrifies the birds in a nearby tree. They explode from the branches in a flurry of coos, dripping feathers. The shriek terrifies the nag. She rears up on her hind legs and screams in alarm. Finally, the shriek terrifies the old man. He's clutching the Rose so tight that his hands bleed. He has also voided the contents of his bladder.

It takes every ounce of the Man within the Beast to restrain him. Blood-red fills his field of vision. He can taste the coppery tang of the liquid in his throat. Meat. The elderly man is meat. But this aspect of himself has been restrained. He gnashes against the psychic tether.

He becomes aware of the mewling man. "Please . . . sir . . . please spare me . . ."

The fear is pathetic. He really should rip out the man's throat. It would be a mercy, really.

"Why should I 'spare' you?" he finds himself saying.

"I am just an old man. A fool. I acted before I thought . . . my wife and my mother say I do so all the time . . ." He's stuttering, and ragged breaths cut up his sentences into jagged pieces. "I saw this miraculous flower, and thought . . . You see, my son, my only child, he has a bit of a green thumb. My trip to the city did not go so well . . . I thought to give him a gift . . ."

"The rosebush will never put forth another bloom. Nothing you can offer will replace it."

"But— but— sir . . ."

The blood-tide rises again. The Beast has been unleashed, free to rend. He leaps from the cover, over the fence with a sinuous grace. He lands on all fours before the cowering man.

He raises a clawed paw, ready to strike. And stops.

He sees himself in the blue mirror of the old man's eye, in all of his terrible glory. He sees a vicious thing, neither dog nor weasel, but somehow both. A long snake-like body, with four legs that ends in razor-sharp claws. A muzzle that slavers, full of serrated teeth. All of this murderous-impulse-made-flesh enrobed in matted golden fur, full of bristles. The man's eyes are as evil and damning as the Mirror in the House.

Perhaps Mercy stops the killing. Mercy, mingled with self-loathing.

"I will spare you," he finds himself saying. The elderly man opens his eyes.

"You are too kind." He is weeping; the Beast does not like this. Water spills from the human's eyes, surely a sign of illness.

Tears. Those are tears. The voice is a whisper, deep within his cursed body. Sometime, years ago, the other that he was, the human, cried tears. Tears of sorrow, tears of frustration, tears of joy.

"Be gone," the Beast says, "before I change my mind."

The Beast slinks back to the garden. He hears the man preparing to leave his house. There is still time to punish the old fool, who thoughtlessly destroyed the one thing in the Beast's long, long life that was beautiful.

The old fool still speaks, even as he gallops away: ". . . I am sorry for the pain I have caused. I will send my son. Perhaps he can ease your . . . affliction."

But the human within is now smothered by the Beast's sorrow. Words have no meaning now.

The Rose was the one thing that that gave him comfort. It is gone, now. All beauty is gone.

When the moon rises, the Beast sings, a pure note of pain that frightens all who hear it.

Years ago, before there was a Beast, there was a young man named Aloysius.

Aloysius lived in the House with his family in comfort and warmth, if not in wealth. The family did well enough. The family business was the cultivation of herbs, some for cooking, but mostly for medicines that apothecaries and the occasional wise woman used. His sisters, three in number and all older than he, married off and vanished to make their own homes when he was quite young. His father groomed him to take over the family business, teaching him a little herb-lore, along with the more practical methods of preserving and storing the plants. His mother was the financial manager of the operation, in addition to keeping the house and the herb garden in good working order.

Life for Aloysius had already been mapped out. It was ordered and predictable. And knowing no better, he could not imagine a greater happiness. When his parents died (the father before the mother), he knew what to do. His grief was deep, but in the end, his parents' knowledge helped him through. Not only did the hard work distract him from lingering sadness, it also made the connection to his parents stronger. The business, after all, was their legacy to him.

His predicable but pleasant life was upended one night. During the harvest season, he hired a few hands to help out. Aloysius had been preparing a late supper when he heard someone rooting about the garden. He thought it might be one of these hands; they tended to be a boisterous, rowdy bunch—jovial and unreliable. He'd had trouble with their sort before. He stepped out of the house, into the night. Before he spoke, he saw something that would forever alter his life.

Aloysius' family, while observant of religion, were rationalists. His father considered himself a kind of dilettante herbalist, and every now and then would offer medical tinctures and potions to the locals. His mother read a steady diet of books about science and the natural world. Many of their neighbors, however, held superstitious beliefs. Spiritism and various occult ventures were quite popular among the gentry; every other major party featured a seance for a while. The peasants had coarser beliefs, of devils, were-beings, and fair folk. Both of his parents frowned on such beliefs. He recalled a time when one of his sisters, Clothilde, had been invited to such a party, and the flurry of tears that fell when she was denied attendance by her parents.

What he saw now was closer to the peasant end of the supernatural spectrum. A Being of Light stood in his front garden. He could not tell if the being was male or female. At first, he thought it was an angel, but it had no wings. The being was quite tall, maybe seven feet or so, and bald. Its skin was transparent, a sort of glass-flesh. Through the glass skin, tiny scintillant jewels coursed in lazy snowflake spirals. These jewels glowed, in an array of colors—sapphire, emerald, ruby, and points in-between. It was nude, or appeared to be. It faced away from him, and gently, sensually worked with something that Aloysius could barely see through the brilliant iridescence. But gradually, the being of light moved, allowing a glimpse of the thing it was working with—a long-dead rose bush that he had been going to remove in the next week or so. The being stroked the bush as if it were a beloved pet. And the bush shivered in response, a silently purring botanical feline. Aloysius stayed silent, bewitched by the alien grace of the being. How long did the creature pluck and prune the bush? He could not say. But at one point, the being glanced toward the sky, and seemed to listen for some sign, its head atilt. Whatever it was listening for apparently answered, for in a starburst flash, it vanished.

Aloysius stood in the doorway for a long time. He was frozen. Fear had turned his blood to ice. Only when dawn crept along the horizon did he stir. He went straight towards the rose bush. Cautiously, he touched it. Nothing had changed, save one thing: it was no longer dead. Where the creature had fondled the plant, a single young bud had sprouted.

Every night, for a week, he stayed up, waiting for the being's reappearance. It did not come back. He made sure that the bush was well watered.

After two weeks had passed, Aloysius took a trip to visit Marie-Chantal, the local wise-woman. She lived in thatched cottage an hour's horse ride outside the village. She was feeding her chickens when his horse entered the clearing. She watched him silently as he tied up the horse.

"Greetings, Marie-Chantal," he said, unsure of the proper address. Did she even have a surname? He had never heard it, nor of a husband.

She was old, her face weathered, browned, and wrinkled. Several skin tags fell down her chin, not unlike the wattles of the chickens that pecked at her feet. She had a faint mustache that was pure black, in contrast to the blue-gray hairs that escaped from her bonnet. But her amber eyes were bright with intelligence, and there was something, maybe in her demeanor, that belied her hag-like appearance.

"Greetings, sir," she replied. Her voice was light and sweet. "What brings you here?"

This was the tricky part. Aloysius sighed, and said, "I have to ask your . . . *expertise* on a matter."

She waited for him to continue.

"A . . . supernatural matter."

"Get on with it, boy. I won't tell."

He told her about the transparent being, and the rosebush while Marie-Chantal mucked out the chicken coop. When he finished, she continued her filthy work for a good five minutes in silence. Aloysius waited impatiently for a response.

She finished, and leaned on the rake she'd been using.

"Your papa wasn't a believer. Thought that the old ways were nonsense. It's true, they are dying out. The roads and ways into this world, and out of it are closing up. Indeed. But every now and then . . . His mother, your gran, however, *was* a believer. She had a touch of the Sight. She'd come to me quite frequently, complaining of noises and lights. She'd see things, much like you described, out in the garden. Angels, she sometimes called them. Demons, other times. I would make a tea for her that would dull her Sight. I think you have inherited her Sight."

Aloysius never knew his grandmother. She'd died before he was born. But he heard stories about her eccentricity. How she would talk to things that no-one could see, and how superstitious she was.

His own mother told a story about how she had strange, repetitive rituals. She had to wash and dry her hands exactly twelve times. The door lock had to be checked sixteen times before they could leave for church. And she spread salt in front of the door and the fireplace. He had just thought she'd been mad.

"Here's an important bit of information, Aloysius," Marie-Chantal said. "You must never, ever let them see you watching them."

"What happens?"

She leaned in close to his face. "Terrible things."

He didn't press her on this issue. He asked other things, instead. "What, exactly, was that creature? And what was it doing with my rose bush?"

Marie-Chantal had the oddest reaction to this line of questioning. She turned as red as the beets that grew in her garden. "Don't make me say, young sir."

It took a few moments—long moments—before Aloysius final figured out what she was alluding to. He turned red as she, sputtering out, "It was *pleasuring* my rose bush? Why on earth would it do that?"

"Who knows? The ways of those folk are decidedly not the ways of folk of flesh and bone. They have different rhythms, and appetites. I think that they would find our ways of—pleasuring ourselves—to be quite base and crass. But I couldn't say. All I can say is this: heed my warning. They are not kind to those with Sight."

A year passed after that meeting. Aloysius mostly forgot the visitation. Only the rosebud, which strangely didn't bloom, was a reminder. He became too busy with his work to think about it. His business grew, and he began getting orders from foreign countries; he had to travel, sometimes abroad. Additionally, he began courting a couple of suitable women, the daughters of the local gentry. His heart wasn't up to the task. The brief, loveless affairs ended affably. As a result, it became easier and easier to view his encounter with the spectral being as some kind of dream, brought on by stress and sorrow.

The autumn harvest came and went, along with the temporarily hired field hands. The farm was empty and silent after that flurry of activity. In a way, he embraced it. He needed to be alone with his thoughts. His mind raced when he lay down for sleep. He got up about five minutes later, planning to have a drink—warm milk laced with alcohol—to ease him into slumber. He found that the kitchen was alight, despite having quaffed the lanterns an hour ago. The light came from outside.

He opened the door, which faced the front end of the house, to investigate. The light came from the rose bush. A pure, golden light. Cautiously, he approached the bush, silently wishing that he wasn't quite so alone. Then he saw what cast that honeyed glow.

The rosebud had bloomed. But 'bloomed' was an inadequate word. The flower was *ablaze*. Each petal burned with the light of a summer sun. It was a velvet flame that spiraled into itself, endlessly. Aloysius's eyes watered at the beauty. His heart felt as bright as the flower shone. He stood looking at this miraculous rose—this Rose (it surely warranted a capital letter) for a long while.

When time had passed, maybe thirty minutes or an hour, he turned and began walking towards the house. He was tired, after all. Maybe the Rose's beauty had overwhelmed him physically as well as spiritually.

A flash, like an exclamation point, burst behind him. And there was the gentlest of disturbances. Soft, like moth wings.

Aloysius turned back around, knowing what he would see. And he did see it.

The ethereal being had returned. It did not see him; it was looking at the Rose, inspecting its handiwork. All of the tiny jewels that made up its inner organs pulsed.

The voice of Marie-Chantal came back to him: *Never let them see you!*

The being was so beautiful, and the Rose was so marvelous, that Aloysius's heart filled with some alien emotion that threatened to burst forth. The feeling spread down to his loins. And he knew then the name of that emotion. He had never felt it before. It was searing his throat. And it escaped from him, in a single

"Oh."

That fell from his lips.

The creature turned and faced him. Its eyes, much like the jewels that swam in its body, changed color frequently. They were now an agitated fuchsia color. Aloysius saw within the dome of its head a jellyfish-like thing floating around, perhaps the being's brain or soul.

This too was vivid fuchsia. Aloysius couldn't control himself. Impulsively, he pressed his lips the creature's lips.

They were neither cold nor warm. The lips were waxy and also hard, like granite. The waxy-stone lips parted, and Aloysius felt breath pass through into his own mouth.

Cinnamon,

the airless gulf between the stars,

the glint of cold silver,

the abrasion of mosquito wings,

the piercing note of a castrato singer,

royal jelly,

molten rock singe,

carapaced beetles burrowing in pig droppings and mud

The kiss was all of these things at once. He found that he couldn't make sense of it, or himself, his flesh, his soul. The breath of the being infused Aloysius, down to the cells and atoms. The breath-mist enveloped his interior, and began destroying him. He felt every cell annihilate and as it died, he was ignited by a kind of spiritual orgasm. Each tiny death ended in a glorious rebirth. Slowly and endlessly, he was reshaped by that breath, cut and scraped and chiseled by a thousand sparkling jewels. The pleasure was so intense that time became meaningless.

He must have fallen asleep after that joining. He lay on the grass. What was his name? It had been taken away from him. Nameless, he stood. And found that he could not. He tried, and succeeded this time, except that his relationship to the ground was different somehow. It was closer to him. His stomach barely went above the grass. And furthermore, his stomach was longer than he remembered it being.

What was this? He found himself lurching forward on four legs. He could see the front two. They were like hands, and not like hands at all. The bone structure of a hand-like thing was there, but it was covered in a golden fur, and each "finger" was tipped with long, claw-like nails. He ran through the grasses, assaulted by the olfactory detonations of scent as vivid as color. Every smell had a layer, a depth, that it hadn't had before. He could easily spend hours, sussing out and exploring the new world of scent, but there was some urgent instinct in him. Something about the house. So he trotted through fields of lavender, rosemary, thyme, henbane, and sage until he reached the house.

Once inside, he found the ground of this dwelling to be difficult to walk upon; his claws scraped the—

The word *floor* floated up from somewhere.

Another word for the wooden hill-things also beckoned, phantasmally. *Stairs*. Up them, he crawled.

When he finally reached the destination, it all became clearer. These smells, this room—he recognized them. The place where he slept. The chamber pot where he voided himself. It was all familiar, but somehow different. There, in one corner of the room, something sparkled, and cast a glowing aura on the ceiling. He approached it, cautiously, sniffing metal and mercury. He glanced into the thing that was like a pool of silver water.

What he saw in this vertical pool was impossible. It was horrible.

A creature stared back at him. It had a tapered snout with fangs that glittered evilly when the mouth was open. It walked on four legs, and each foot ended in cruel claws. Rams' curled horns sprouted from its awful head. The body of the beast was long, rather like a weasel's body. This body was covered in thick, blond fur. Neither ram nor weasel nor lynx— it was all three. A monster. An abomination.

Don't let them see you.

A Beast.

Marie-Chantal's warning came back to him. What a fool he had been. He should have heeded her. The Being had cursed him for his impropriety.

The human within him still had the upper hand. He didn't know how long that would last. Things were slipping away from him, already. For instance, his name. The bestial side of him wanted to flee from this strange waterless pool and hunt. Already, visions of gouting blood and fresh meat filled his brain. It was with intense concentration that he formulated a plan. It was rudimentary: find the wise-woman and—

Someone was in the house. He smelled them before he heard them. A male, human, middle aged, stinking of sweat, soap, and beer. The human brayed. It spoke. For a moment, the Beast seemed to understand the inane braying sounds, sounds that conjured images.

"Monsieur Aloysius," said the human prey. "Are you in?"

This human was familiar. It had a name, that was lost. Instinctively, the Beast moved toward the sound. It slunk, close to the ground. It was stalking. The arrangement of muscles, where and when to step, what shape the body made against the different terrain—it all made marvelous sense. It felt right.

"Sir?" squawked the human male.

The Beast huddled in a knot of shadow in front of the door where the human male bumbled around. The male was messing about with crockery, helping himself to some liquid refreshment. He stopped, sensing eyes on him. The human gazed into the darkness with his inferior eyes.

"Master—?"

The Beast pounced, and landed in the room. The human dropped his mug of beer and screamed. The moment to kill came. Now! But, the Beast paused. The stench of familiarity made the prey less appetizing. Besides, the blood in this one was sweet and sluggish with illness. A snarl, the raising of hackles: these things sent the human on its way, gracelessly. Enraged and frustrated, the Beast lifted its leg, and let pour forth a pungent stream of urine. This cave was *his*.

Time passed; he wasn't sure of the length. Beasts don't measure time. They live in the ever-present Now. Sun and moon, waking and sleeping are the only markers. It was deep in the woods one day, feasting on the steaming entrails of a freshly slaughtered doe when the stink of man invaded his nostrils. Then he heard them, their ridiculous squawking noises.

It was two women winding through the woods in a short cut. They chattered like birds. The Beast slunk down in the bracken.

"I hear the place is cursed," said one of the females.

"Genevieve, you surprise me. I didn't think you were one for silly gossip," said the elder female.

"Oh, this is no idle talk, Mona. I heard it straight from Claude's lips. An eye-witness account."

"You mean that drunken fool?"

"Come now—Claude is loyal and sweet, and he has never been one to tell tales. He told me about an encounter with some hideous creature at Master Aloysius's farm when I stopped in the Cockatrice for a small draught. He looked downright disturbed, sulking over his beer. I greeted him, but he seemed so . . . morose. I asked him what was the matter. He turned from his beer mug, and his face was as white as farmer's cheese. He said, 'I know it killed him. It killed and ate him up.' I asked Marthe, what's he going on about? And she says, Claude's been muttering about it for a week, something a weird beast in the Villier's farm. At this point, Claude interrupted blearily. 'I know what I saw. A beast. An unnatural thing, not wolf nor ram nor stoat. Horned, it was, with the fangs of a wild cat. It would have killed me, but it was probably full from its first meal: Master Aloysius. And then he begins blubbing like a baby!"

The human within the Beast stirred, remembering its long-forgotten plan. The Beast waited until the women continued on their way. When he could no longer smell them, he began the trek to the wise woman's home. He forgot her name, but knew what she looked like. Though the Beast moved much quicker than a man, the trip was constantly waylaid by the Beast's nature. A darting hare, or dallying pheasant would distract the monster, stimulating the hunting instinct. It took every bit of concentration not to succumb to base desires. It was evening before he smelled the familiar stink of goats, chicken, herbs and human female.

The wise woman was outside, feeding her fowl, and singing some wordless melody. The gloaming had descended in tones of gold, rose, and dusky blue. The Beast waited. It was struggling with itself. The human was trying to find language, while the Beast was trying to remember the taste of goat flesh. He sat deep in the cover, hidden by bushes and upwind so the animals wouldn't notice him. It got darker as he observed the tableaux, which could end either with fear or violence. Presently, the wise woman stopped singing.

She stayed silent for a minute or two. He recognized the stance of a fellow stalker. She was listening. But for what? She uttered a word of Power, one that crackled with electricity. The world plunged into silence. The goats, chickens, and songbirds stopped their sounds. The wise woman turned, glanced this way, that. She stood still, her gaze landing on the patch of brush where he lay hiding.

She said, "What manner of thing are you? Reveal yourself." The words itched and tingled; it was as if a thousand fleas swarmed over his hide. He had no choice but to obey the old female. The Beast was inflamed with rage. He crawled out of the brush sullenly.

The woman gasped at his appearance. He snarled at her in reply.

She said, "You are unnatural. That much is sure." The goats and chickens saw him as well, and they started a racket of distressed calls. She said to them, "Calm down, darlings. I won't let you come to harm."

"If you can speak, do so." This was yet another command, inlaid with Power that he could not resist.

The human within him woke, regaining the upper hand. Forming words, however, was difficult. The anatomy of the Beast's muzzle was not made for speaking. The sounds that emerged were partially growls and purrs.

"Free me, bitch. So I can rip your throat out."

The wise woman smiled. "Now, now. No more naughty language. Or there will be consequences."

He swore at her.

The woman made no visible gesture, but at once he was engulfed in pain. It was exquisite, a filigree tracery of wire-thin burning throughout his entire body. His awareness of the world shrunk, until he was only aware of agony.

When it finally subsided, the old woman said, "Let's try this again, shall we? Who are you?"

A word untethered itself from somewhere deep within. A sound that was a symbol, was sentience itself. "I am Aloysius Villier."

"Sweet mother of God," she said. Her hands rose to her mouth as if they wanted to contain the shock she felt.

"How did you— What happened?" She sputtered out the words.

The Beast, or rather, Aloysius-in-the-Beast, told her the story of his encounter with the transparent creature.

"I thought I told you not to let it see you. What made you kiss the damned thing?"

"I could not help myself. It was so beautiful."

The wise woman frowned at him. "You should never touch, let alone kiss, another without getting their consent."

The Beast had nothing to say to this.

Marie-Chantal continued: "Well, what's done is done"

"Can you help me? Turn me back to the way I was?"

Her face struck a thoughtful cast. After a while, she said, "I'll be honest, Aloysius. This is beyond my power's scope. Bringing down a fever is one thing; shape-shifting is quite another. The best I can do is beg an audience with the fairy who cursed you so."

"I thought fairies were tiny things with moth wings."

"There's different types of fairies, just as there are different types of folk. In Cathay, the folk are golden-yellow. In Africa, the men and women have dark skin and wooly black tufts of hair. But, enough about that! I recall a spell my grandmother told me that might summon the thing. No, stay where you are. My hold on your bestial nature will weaken while I perform the enchantment. I need you far enough away in case that spell ends."

She closed her eyes, and began singing some dreadful tuneless melody. Aloysius felt himself drowning in the swirl of beastliness. Though he was partially submerged, the irrational rage was still somewhat contained. Meanwhile, the melody sped up, with the words becoming harsher and harsher. Spit flecked from her lips at particularly guttural junctures.

Spell-casting is an ugly business, he thought.

As if to underscore that point, the air thickened around Marie-Chantal and blurred her form behind a greasy film. There was the odor of burning, too. What was burning? Perhaps the very ozone itself, as a doorway was carved from this world, leading into the other. The wise woman's song devolved into full-on shrieking; Marie-Chantal sounded as if she were shredding her vocal cords. There was a final cry, at which point a void appeared where odd blurring was. An oval of pure darkness. It hovered in front of Marie-Chantal, like a demented black moon. The blackness was inert. What substance was the blackness? Both Beast and human cowered instinctively.

A queer silence descended. Even the wind stopped, listening and waiting. Then:

Something emerged from the void, something with crystal skin and marvelous blobs of color whirling within it. Aloysius could not tell if this was the same being or not. Despite its graceful movements, it looked disoriented, as if it had been woken up from a deep sleep.

Marie-Chantal bowed before the Being, then knelt.

"Oh, noble sir. Or madame. I beg your pardon a thousand times for disturbing you."

It lazily glanced down at her. The expression It wore was a cross between contempt and amazement. As if Marie-Chantal were a kind of animal who had suddenly gained the ability to speak.

When it spoke, Aloysius heard its voice in his head. Words and concepts simply appeared in his mind, with the glittery precision of diamonds.

-*Why hast thou called me, creature of meat and hair?*

Marie-Chantal still knelt, and answered looking at the ground. "Fairest one, I beg a favor you."

A look of annoyance crossed its face. The whirling bits of color turned to an awful shade of yellow, like rotten egg yolks.

-*Get on with it, then.*

Marie-Chantal wetted her lips. She said, "A few days ago, a foolish man assaulted you with his—impertinence. He knew no better. Rightfully, you rebuked him. I beg your mercy, fairest one. Can you not grant clemency in this matter, and return to him his rightful form?"

The Being looked up into the gloaming air, and appeared to sniff it. It spun around, and faced the Beast directly. The gaze it laid upon him was as fierce as it was alien. Aloysius could not read it.

-*Dear hag, that is his rightful form. I* gifted *him with this shape. His essence is encased in splendid fur and gold.*

"Um. Er. So I see, fair one. He is, indeed, a most marvelous creature. However. We humans—we creatures of meat and hair, as you put it so poetically—must interact with each other, and the form you gave him—excuse me—*gifted* him with—will him cause much complication."

The Being rolled its eyes.

-*Is this your desire, to return to your awkward mortal shape?*

"It is," said Aloysius.

The Being suddenly appeared before him. Aloysius found himself rising on his hind legs. When he was level with the Being's face, it grasped him by the scruff of his neck and kissed him.

A silvery, perfumed breath went down his throat. It carried within it one of the ever-changing jewels. Aloysius felt this ghost gem descend and lodge somewhere in his guts.

The kiss ended.

-*There. I have done my part. The Seed of Change is within you. You must awaken it.*

The air ignited with a thousand scintillant jewels which were in turn swallowed by a formless darkness.

It was dawn when the Beast regained consciousness. The surrounding clouds were bloody with morning light. And the area around him matched this with blood of its own. There was the corpse of a woman nearby. Her throat had been torn out. The Beast felt something strange in its guts. Something that had no real name in the animal way of life, some vestige of his human self. Guilt, mixed with a hint of sorrow. It seemed that the human within him knew this woman, who had doubtlessly threatened the Beast in some way. The act of murder itself, the Beast could not recall. Faint images wisped by in his brain—a dark portal, some kind of creature. It was irrelevant to the Beast, who only needed to survive.

The Beast sat on his hind legs, and howled to the bloody sun. It screamed away the last vestiges of humanity with baleful note. When the song finished, he loped away from the scene.

Years passed. But, of course, time had no meaning to the creature of fur and gold. An hour was a year. A moment could last forever.

There was always the thrill of the hunt to occupy him. It was a dance of shadow and blood. But for the most part, the human within in was submerged in the Beast. Only the Rose awakened the human, briefly at night before sleep overtook him.

The Villier estate fell into disrepair, and the herb gardens went to seed. Every now and then, some person might pay the grounds a visit, not hearing of the various local rumors that abounded in the countryside. For the most part, they were greeted with a decrepit building, with the furniture shrouded in dust. But every now and again, an adventurous soul might hear something lurking in the upper levels or a distant room, or else, catch a glimpse of fur or fang through the now riotous garden. As a result, the house and grounds became to be known as haunted or cursed.

The audience with the fairy was long forgotten, smothered like the human soul in a cloud of bestial desires.

¤

Since the Rose is gone, the Beast no longer has any tie his former shape. He no longer sleeps in the House; he did so out of habit, perhaps. Instinct leads him to more suitable settlements. He might not glance at the House for days or even weeks.

But one evening, after a bloody meal of deer, he ranges back to the garden and sees a light coming from the House. It is not a natural light, like the sun and the moon, nor is it a reflective trick of glass. No. This light is yellow and wavering. It is a flame. The Beast hunkers down and slides through the lanes of lavender and coriander. As he does so, there is smell drifting in the air. The smell of cooked meat wafts by. That, and the burning of wood.

A rage stirs in the Beast's heart, as fiery as the blaze that is in the House. Though he no longer lives there, the House belongs to the Beast. It has been marked with urine and feces, odorous warnings that stake his claim on this territory. The rage simmers down. He must be stealthy, and observe the habits of this new invader, and discover it's vulnerability.

The Beast settles in for a night, lightly dozing in the brush. When dawn blooms, there's a creak as the front door to the House opens. Out steps a young man—a most unusual human. His skin is dusky, and his hair is like black wool. His lips are thick and purple, the color of wine. He is dressed in simple-but-well-made clothes. He scans the front garden, then the back. Surely, his eyes cannot pierce the shadow and find the Beast's shape. And yet—the Beast wishes that this man's eyes *would* fall upon him. The fire in the Beast's heart then moves to a most curious place. For some reason, he is reminded of the Rose. The intruder is at least as beautiful as that flower.

Once the man is satisfied that no-one else is around, he bends down and sets a bowl upon the porch, then goes back into the House.

The bowl is full of meat that had been lightly cooked. The Beast can smell it from his hiding place. His mouth waters at the scent, which is irresistible. But the Beast is not hungry; raw venison fills his belly. As a result, the scent of cooked meat triggers another thing, as alien and unwanted as the invader in the House.

Memory. *Human* memory.

Aloysius awakes, stirred by the olfactory mnemonic. The Beast subsides, sullenly, as the man's consciousness takes over. It comes back to him, in bursts of images. Marie-Chantal. The Ethereal Being's curse and subsequent rescinding of that curse. And the merchant, and his promise to send his son.

Aloysius now has his name back.

The transformation has begun.

And most importantly, he knows how to end the spell.

Black-Winged Roses

The woman was no great beauty, not by a long shot. In fact, she was downright ugly. Junkyard dog ugly. She was short, with a large behind and top heavy to boot. Her skin was not smooth. It was interrupted by discolorations, where she was darker around her eyes like a damned raccoon. Her nose was wide, and her lips were thick and liver-colored. But her hair was the worst thing about her, the icing on the hideous cake. It was unprocessed, wild and wooly, in thick tufts.

Madame Isis wanted to sing out "baa baa black sheep" to this poor country girl. At least the girl had bothered to stick a rose in her hair. It looked like the rose was growing from her head. She was also reasonably outfitted in a dark blue dress, black stockings, earrings the same color as the dress, and white lace gloves.

"Miss Lady," said Madame Isis from her seat in front of the small stage, "this here is an audition for *pianists*. Not for singers." She motioned the dark girl off the stage.

"I know that," the ugly thing had the nerve to reply. With attitude. "I *am* a pianist."

Madame Isis scowled at her. "This ain't a church, darling. Do you know what kind of club this is?"

"I ain't blue nosed," she said. Her voice was raspy. It crackled like mesquite. "I know perfectly well what kind of folk this club caters to." This answer satisfied Madame Isis; on second glance, the girl was probably a femme. The dark girl surveyed the club from her perch on the stage. Madame Isis cringed internally. The Ankh Club had seen better days, it was true. The tables were scored and tattooed with the imprint of a thousand drinks, and the chandelier was missing a few crystals. The black and white floor tile was filthy and scuffed. It was only her and Jasper, who served as doorman, barkeep, and security. "May I play you something?"

Madame Isis produced a cigarette from some hidden pocket in her gown and snapped her fingers. Jasper emerged from the shadows, ostensibly to light it. The young man frantically patted himself down, looking for a lighter. This inconvenience was really the last straw. It had been a simply awful day. She had woken up with a pounding headache. Horus, her cat, had thrown up on one of her gowns, and on her way to the club, some wiseacre had the nerve to call her a "she-male" right in the street, in front of an audience of upright church ladies. The auditions had gone abysmally, a procession of incompetent players parading (and, in one case, stumbling) across the stage. She was about to snap at Jasper, who should have known better, when the dark girl glided over to her (with more grace than Madame Isis thought possible) and lit her cigarette in one smooth motion.

She thanked the lady pianist after taking a deep drag from her cigarette, and gave her consent for her to play. The woman sat at the battered Steinway and played "Summertime," a fairly straightforward rendition with some minor key flourishes. Though she didn't sing, the lyrics' story played through Madame Isis's mind like scenes from a motion picture. She saw the faded splendor of Catfish Row, smelled the sludgy, fishy air of the Cooper River. Each ornamental riff clarified the images in her head. Brown faces sweating beneath a Southern sun, the heat-haze that rose from the river. Then the song ended. The dark girl paused a beat, waiting for a reaction. Isis motioned for the girl to continue. "Gloomy Sunday" was the next song. The pianist summoned the black coach of sorrow itself, squeaky wheels and all.

Madame Isis tried to come up with a reason not to hire the young woman. While the young woman was talented, the performers at the Ankh Club had to exude a certain glamour. Cakeboys and bulldaggers liked women to be elegant, fine-featured, and light-skinned, like Lena Horne, and not like their dark-skinned country cousin from Down South.

The song changed again, to an upbeat boogie-woogie number. That's when Madame Isis saw them. A crowd of people were in the room with her. The men and women all had the same dazed look on their faces, as if someone had surprised them with flash photography. Their clothes were washed out, and their skin held no luster.

Try as she might, Madame Isis couldn't see their faces. She saw eyes, mouths, and noses. Smiles, and laugh-lines. But she couldn't hold their shapes in her mind. Her cigarette smoke curled around the group's faces and bodies. And the smoke went through them.

Madame Isis dropped her cigarette the same time the song ended. The young woman finished playing, and stood. The crowd vanished, celluloid figures fading to black.

"What is your name, darling?" she found herself asking.

"I am Etta Mae Watson," the dark girl replied.

"Oh no. That will never do," said Madame Isis. "You will have to come up with a stage name."

A month later, the Ankh Club was busy. Negroes even lined up to get in. Word spread quickly about this lady pianist, who called herself Coalrose. She was a natural performer. Though she wasn't much to look at, you couldn't keep your eyes off her. That Saturday night, she wore a pale lavender pantsuit, silver strap heels and a string of pearls around her neck. This time, there were three black roses growing in her hair. She played songs by Count Basie, Cab Calloway, and Scott Joplin. She even sang sometimes. Her voice was deep and quavering, like a clarinet. Bulldaggers, fairies, butches, queens, and all points in between responded to "Coalrose's" music. During the sexy songs, they made out, and caressed each other in frenzied fits. People openly wept during the ballads. And during particularly acrobatic keyboard work, people shouted out, like folks who got the spirit in church.

Madame Isis knew she was a conjure woman. She could practically see the mojo radiating off Coalrose. Every gesture had unspent energy, waiting to burst free. Every note she sang was an uncast spell. Coalrose siphoned off the mood of the crowd and flung it back to them, transformed into something new. Madame Isis knew she had mojo, because she once had it herself. Back when she was young, Azalea, the coastal southern town she had grown up in, was famous for its low country cuisine, its profusion of namesake bushes, and the sheer number of its conjure folk. Mother Lightning had taught her how to speak to the dead, and to those spirits who had never been housed in flesh. Aunt Junebug taught her how to heal, and how to curse. And Brother Creek revealed her true self, trapped in a boy's body, and taught her how to cast glamours. Her teachers trained her well, until she became skilled herself. The problem was that Coalrose didn't know that she had mojo.

Mother Lightning told her, "It's a good thing you sought us out. Ain't nothing more dangerous than a gifted one throwing charms with no guidance. All sorts of mischief can happen."

The departed winked into existence, making the subterranean club seem even more crowded. The men and women wore faded, out-of-date outfits, like cloche hats or had konked hairstyles. They all wore the same bemused expressions when they manifested, as if they had just woken up from a deep sleep. They wandered around the club, weaving between tables and people who for the most part, ignored them. But every now and then one of the patrons *did* see them, and gasped at the haints. Poor Jasper was one of the people who could see them. He kept trying to serve them drinks, only to be ignored. The other bar customers were understandably confused. "Is you talking to me?" they asked the harried bartender. When Coalrose went on break, the haints vanished, like blue smoke. When she returned to the stage, they reappeared, glittering eyes focused on the performer.

When the club closed at three in the morning, the haints were nowhere to be found. But Madame Isis knew that they were still in the club, attracted by the residual magic.

It didn't take long for Coalrose's mojo to cause trouble. It was inevitable. The Ankh Club was underground, for obvious reasons. Morals raids were always a threat. Madame Isis had lived through several of them. For the most part, though, the Fuzz avoided Harlem, and busting fairies and dykes was not high on their list of priorities. As long as they stayed below notice, there would be no trouble. Many of the residents of their neighborhood knew of the club's existence, and to whom it catered. The occasional tough guy might harass the clientele, but most folk had a "see no evil, hear no evil" demeanor and let them sin in peace.

Jeremiah Black, however, searched for sin like it was his life's work. He sniffed it out like a bloodhound on the trail of a fugitive.

He was a big man, at least six foot and built like an ox. His skin was so dark that his teeth and the whites of his eyes were as yellow as lemons. He always wore the same undertaker's suit and black trilby, his thick hair oozing out of the sides. He would stand on street corners, preaching his own warped view of the Scripture. His street name was *Jeremiad* Black.

Most people tuned him out, but every now and then, Jeremiah would get on a real kick, focusing on a pet sin. One summer, he screamed outside of the Apollo, accosting anyone who entered the theater. Another time, he stood in front of the Cotton Club and had to be bodily removed by the security guards, screeching all the while about how the saxophone was the Devil's trumpet.

After that, Jeremiah kind of disappeared. Rumor had it that he had been sent to the Funny Farm. But he came back one Friday afternoon, and his target this time was the Ankh Club. Someone had tipped him off to the location. In the past, Madame Isis had juju-based wards in place to confuse and repel interlopers. Now, the club was unprotected.

"There is a nest of Sodomites operating in the heart of our God-fearing neighborhood," he shouted. He stood at the entrance of the alley where the door to the Ankh Club was. "Men laying with men. Women kissing women. Defiling the sanctity of the Word with their vile, foul rituals!"

There was a small crowd of people gathered around him, blocking her way in. She thought that most of them were probably rubberneckers, eager for a confrontation. But she had seen people riled up by demagogues, people who were normally sweet natured. Aunt Junebug had been run out of Azalea by people riled up by Preacher Frame once, people who used Aunt Junebug's services.

Once blood was in the water, anything could happen.

She stayed out of the sightline of Jeremiah, out in the street where there was traffic. Madame Isis usually arrived at the club in the late afternoon to get some work done and greet performers and vendors. Maybe Jeremiah and his crowd would disperse sometime soon. She stepped into Eubie's, the corner coffeeshop, and found that Jasper was sitting at the counter sipping a cup of joe.

"Is he still there?" he asked her when she sat down.

"Yes. Let's give them a few more minutes. The crowd might get bored."

"I hope so," he said. "Coalrose — Etta is stopping by early to practice some new material in an hour."

They watched the clock move slowly as they drank their coffees. Madame Isis no longer had the energy or focus to work mojo. She just had barely enough to maintain her allure. And sometimes, even that light dusting didn't work all the time, and she had to go out in her birth body, as Isaiah. Mostly, Isis was tired all the time, but she couldn't properly rest. Every room was too cold, even in high summer. And her memory faded. Names of relatives, old lovers, past enchantments, the properties of herbs—all slipped from her mind like sand through a sieve. She tried writing things down, but she always lost the notepad or the pencil. Back in the day, she had been a force to reckon with. She stood seven feet tall in heels, and wore dramatic outfits that telegraphed her presence. Feathered headdresses, brightly patterned wraps, outfits in lamé and moiré, accentuating baubles of turquoise, topaz, carmine, and onyx. Now she was lucky if she could afford velveteen. She no longer wore heels; her sense of balance was precarious. Once, she could feel the earth beneath the pavement when she walked in stilettos and pumps. The tug of gravity, the heat-death of the buried and forgotten, and the calibration of the tectonic plates all coursed through her veins. Now, she wore ballet flats and only felt the aching of her joints.

The hour was up quickly. She and Jasper left Eubie's and headed for the alley. She could hear old Jeremiah still at it. This was going to get ugly. Isis was too old for this shit. She should have been an honored elder, and not still be fighting the same battles over and over. At least she had Jasper. Jasper, however, was spooked. His eyes were wide, his hands trembled. Though he never really gave her a straight answer about his past, Isis guessed that he, like many of the Ankh Club's patrons, was a prodigal son, cast out and taking refuge in the wicked city. No, Jasper would be useless. She sighed to herself. *Remember, once you were the Goddess-Empress of Harlem.* She pulled herself up to her full six-foot-seven height, ignoring her protesting muscles and spine. She turned the corner.

Unfortunately, Jeremiah's crowd had grown. There were now at least thirty or so people crammed into the alley. She had held onto the slim hope that she could have squeezed past them without engaging, but that would be impossible.

"There he is! The sin-peddler himself," shouted Jeremiah. "Don't be fooled—that's a man underneath that whorish costume. Blasphemer!"

It took all of Isis's resolve not to shudder. Jeremiah shook with righteous anger. She might have been Old Scratch himself.

"Jeremiah Black, don't you have anything better to do than pester hardworking folks," she said. Isis heard the cracks in her voice. "Let us go to work."

"Hush, foul Sodomite! This transvestite owns this den of sin! A place where men and women perform lewd acts that are a mockery of the sacred union!"

"The only acts we perform are musical ones," said Isis. "Your mind is in the gutter, Mister Black."

"*Hebrews 13: Marriage should be honored by all, and the marriage bed kept pure, for God will judge the adulterer and the sexually immoral!*"

"Where's your wife?" Isis shouted back.

"I am doing the Lord's work! I have no need of a helpmeet, you wretched abomination!"

The words scalded Isis. They brought back that frightened little girl that was trapped in a boy's body. Then, Brother Creek's voice cut through the fear like a knife: *You are Isis. Never forget your true name.* She didn't feel like Isis at the moment. She felt like a freak of nature. *There are no freaks of nature,* Brother Creek once told her. *You are a part of nature.* It sounded better when Isis had power at her fingertips.

She said, "Flattery will get you nowhere. If you'll excuse me . . ." The crowd chuckled at that, which enraged Jeremiah further.

"'*A woman shall not wear a man's garments, nor shall a man put on a woman's cloak, for whoever does these things is an abomination to the Lord!*' Deuteronomy 22," he spat out. There was a ripple of applause.

"Abomination coming through," said Madame Isis through gritted teeth, and began to swan her way through the crowd. The gathered folk moved quickly away from Isis and Jasper, as if both were contagious. Jeremiah, however, did not move from his spot, essentially blocking the both of them. Jeremiah was not as tall as Madame Isis. However, he was much stronger and could probably crack her spine. The two of them almost came face to face. She could smell his breath, which was rank with onions.

"Outta my way," she said to him.

There was a deadness in his eyes. To him, Madame Isis was a thing, and not a person. She was the manifestation of evil. She was a weed that needed to be uprooted from Harlem. She was poisonous, a serpent in a gown. She could see in his eyes that he would hurt her, fired up with the wrath of his Lord. She'd been smitten by Bible thumpers before. But in the past, she could fight back. Could Jasper help her? She wasn't so sure. He looked like he was just about to jump out of his skin.

"Stop," she heard the Watson girl say, somewhere behind her.

Jeremiah broke eye contact with Isis. "Who is you?" he asked, "Another she-male?"

Isis turned around to see the girl shaking like a leaf. She wore a tuxedo, altered to fit her frame, and her hair was teased out to its full length, haloing her face.

"Excuse me?" Etta Mae said.

"I said, are you a transvestite? Or are you one of those *unnatural* women?"

Etta Mae said nothing.

"Jeremiah," Isis said. She felt the tension in the air. It was heavy with dark mojo, all coming from the girl. It was radiating from her, like heat, cold, rain, and snow. Isis felt the urge to warn him. That was the good thing to do. Then, she recalled that dead-eyed look he'd given her. The one that had stripped her of her humanity, that turned regal Madame Isis into a frightened little child.

"How dare you," Etta Mae said. Her voice was deeper, the dusky voice from her stage performances. *That* voice crackled with fire, charcoal-dark.

"Hush, woman," said Jeremiah. "And you—" He grabbed Isis's forearm hard. He ripped the turban from her head and threw it into a pile of festering garbage. Isis cringed, both from the vice-like grip and from the shame. Everyone could see that she was balding. "Foul deceiver, false female. This is the pitiful creature that hides behind make-up and whorish baubles . . ."

"You low-down snake," said Coalrose. Madame Isis could see her power writhing around and through her, dark vine-like skeins. "You let her go!"

For one awful moment, nothing happened.

Jeremiah let go of his bruising grip with a cry of pain. Isis saw thorns, piercing his skin and the fabric of his suit. They burst from beneath his skin, dark barbs. His arms and legs undulated. The thorns vanished as quickly as they had sprouted. A look of wild terror etched itself on his features. Then, he bolted from the alley.

And so did Etta Mae Watson.

It took Isis a week, with Jasper's help, to find Etta Mae. She lived in a women's boarding house in the hinterlands of Sugar Hill. People stopped going to the Ankh Club during her disappearance. They went to other underground clubs, like Sappho's, Jade's, and Delany's Place. Isis couldn't blame them—those In the Life had to find each other somehow, and the piers were dangerous and dominated by the white queers. For one, brief shining moment, the Ankh Club had been the crown jewel of the scene. Now, it would fade away, like all of those other watering holes, like the lamented Daffodils, The Flame, and Fairyland. The Ankh Club was the only venue that featured music. For many, it was back to the docks, and back to the shadows.

Isis wore a conservative gray dress that fell below her knees and a white turban. The only jewelry she wore were small ruby studs. She considered wearing a cross, but thought that would be overselling it. She wore Oxford flats, rather than her preferred pumps.

A scowling silver-haired woman opened the door after she rang.

"How may I help you," she said.

"I would like to speak to Etta Mae Watson," said Madame Isis. The woman stood in the door, blocking her.

"Guests must be cleared for visits on Sunday nights. You aren't on the list." The den mother stepped back and began closing the door.

Madame Isis stuck her foot in the door, jamming it. "Let her know that I'm here." She was glad that she wore the Oxfords.

The woman was tiny and couldn't move Isis's foot if she tried. That didn't stop her, though. "Ma'am, I'm going to have to ask you to leave."

Isis busted through, and the woman almost toppled over. "Which room is she in?"

"I'm going to call the police—"

"Miss Dunbar! There's no need to call the authorities." Etta Mae stood on the stairs. She wore a floral dress and white gloves, making her look every inch the country bumpkin. "Miss Derrick, I'll meet you outside. Give me a minute."

Miss Dunbar looked disappointed. She was a born snitch. Isis stood on the brownstone's steps as she waited for Etta Mae Watson to get ready. Old Sourpuss watched her like a hawk. Madame Isis stuck her tongue out at the lady and immediately felt better. Etta Mae came down shortly after, her Afro wrapped in a scarf. She didn't meet Isis's eyes. Instead, she stared at the cracks in the stairs.

"How are you doing?" Madame Isis gently touched the girl's shoulder.

"Okay, I guess," she mumbled. Then she looked up. "I didn't hurt him too bad, did I?"

Madame Isis scoffed. "Child, that man was fixing to kill me. My very existence represents everything he hates about the world, and himself. You didn't hurt him anymore than he hurt himself."

Etta Mae led her to a coffee shop called Java N' Joe. It had clearly been something else quite recently. The damask wallpaper had been hastily painted over. The linoleum was scuffed. And the coffee was awful, full of bitter grounds.

"I can't control it," Etta Mae said. "It just rises up out of me, like a storm. They thought I was the Devil's daughter, back home. Even though I carried a cross and went to church twice a week, things would still happen around me. Once, a small flock of starlings sat by my school window. When I went to the outhouse, they followed me. Then they followed me back into the school. They flew everywhere, and shit on the desks. Another time, I was walking home with my friend Beulah during a sudden thunderstorm. Neither of us got wet, and Beulah's mama forbade her to see me. They called me Coal-black Etta, the bad luck girl. When the Higginbotham's cow had a two-headed calf, guess who they blamed? People started seeing me on the sly, for love charms and hexes. But I didn't want to hurt nobody. I still don't."

Madame Isis took one more swig of the muddy brew. "Coal-black Etta," she said. "I see where Coalrose comes from. You took the weakest part of you, and made it the best part of you."

"What do you mean?"

"You don't know how to control your power. But Coalrose does. *Coalrose* is magic.

"There's a gentleman who comes to all of your shows, named Bucephalus Wilson. Maybe you've seen him. He's a quiet man, light-skinned, gray-haired, balding with a tiny moustache and glasses. He always dresses like he's going to church—in a suit and tie."

"Does he wear a straw hat?"

"Yes! That's him. He is always pleasant, and smiles but never speaks. He doesn't drink and he sits alone, in the same spot, to the left of the stage. Mr. Wilson is pleasant but he's a little . . . *off*, if you know what I mean. He has a vacant stare, and nothing seems to affect him. Like, one time a patron spilled a drink on him. Bucephalus might have blinked. Another time, he might have accidentally stepped on some queen's foot or bumped him. The queen had a fit. Read him the Riot Act, and cursed at him like a drunk sailor. Old Bucephalus just slowly sauntered back to his seat as if nothing had happened."

Etta Mae didn't drink the coffee in her cup. She just swirled it around, watching the silt surface. She avoided Isis's gaze. She seemed to be lost in her own pain.

Madame Isis continued: "Anyway, Jasper found out from one of the regulars what Bucephalus's deal is. You see, he was in Bellevue for a while. A year or two. I don't know how or why he got there. But while he was there, they did an operation on him. They took a part of his brain, or scrambled it. And turned him into a placid, smiling mute. Ever since then, he wasn't quite right.

"Well, when you played 'Nature Boy,' tears fell from his eyes. And I saw him mouth the words. "That's a small miracle. Is that something a Devil's daughter could do?"

One by one, they fell, like toy soldiers or dominoes. Jade's closed due to a moral's raid. It was all over the papers: NEST OF NEGRO PERVERTS SQUASHED! The more salacious papers shared pictures of the disgraced patrons, one of which was an alderman. Delany's Place was embroiled in scandal: a man had been murdered in front of the store that served as the watering hole after-hours. He'd been stabbed through the heart. Weegee had traveled up above 125th to take one of his crime pictures. Isis recognized the victim's face; he'd come to the Ankh Club every now and then. Then there was a bomb threat at Sappho's, and arson was suspected at The Inkwell, one of the newer establishments.

Meanwhile, the Ankh Club's popularity grew. There was a line to get in, and the tiny basement was filled to capacity. A Fire Marshall would have surely closed them down. But the Children came anyway. The club was an oasis, a sanctuary away from the world that hated them. Coalrose had returned to the stage, invigorated and with a new longer name. She was now Zoë Coalrose. Etta Mae Watson was gone, or asleep. Madame Isis loved the new sobriquet. The name rolled off the tongue, resonant with dark magic and negritude. And when she performed on stage, she wove spells out of the gathered crowd's fear and despair. Every note coaxed from the ivories or from the ebony of her voice floated above the crowd like a butterfly, or a bubble. Isis could see it wavering around the ceiling, among the exposed pipes. They were all transfixed—the living and the shadow folk.

The night that Madame Isis swore would be her last, the club was hopping. Saturday at two-thirty on a late autumn night, the club was misty with sweat, and reeked of alcohol. The drinks flowed like the river Jordan, and a crush of folks was up front by the stage, waiting. Bulldaggers had started dressing like Coalrose, in pastel-colored suits, their hair grown natural and wooly. The cakeboys paid tribute to the performer by wearing roses in their lapels. Even Old Bucephalus had pinned a black rose to his vest. Madame Isis wore a long gown of acid green, silver heels and a turban with an ostrich plume. She felt like a queen as she strode through the club, soaking up the residual magic Zoë Coalrose cast out. The set she'd played was full of jaunty tunes, bright and gay as Christmas tree lights. The shadow folk swirled around the crowd, illuminated by cigarette smoke. Madame Isis heard snatches of conversation as she patrolled the realm.

"She's good enough to play the Alhambra Ballroom!"

"Did you see that transparent Negro just a second ago?"

"I hear she and Madame Isis are in a relationship . . ."

She was chuckling at that one when Jasper interrupted her promenade. She immediately knew something was wrong.

"Jeremiah is in the alley again," he said.

The night air was a shock after the tropical warmth of the club. She could hear Jeremiah's screeching, as he hectored the people who were outside smoking. Jeremiah Black was always off, but this time he seemed especially so. His undertaker's suit was no longer clean. It was frayed, with oily stains and bird shit. And he staggered as he walked from each grouping to harangue them with his apocalyptic blather.

"The Witch of Endor resides in this den of inequity! A perverted Delilah, a Whore of Babylon!" The madness rolled off of him in waves. "This She-Devil practices Dark Arts. She hides her spells in song and dance, but make no mistake . . ."

Jeremiah lost his train of thought when he saw Madame Isis outside of the club. He squinted his eyes, and lurched toward her. That's when the smell hit her. The urine stench of gasoline burned her nose. His suit was dripping with the liquid.

"Where is the witch," he said. He grabbed Isis's forearm in the same place he had before.

She tried to wiggle her way out of his grip. "There is no witch, Jeremiah."

He laughed. It was almost a giggle, it was that giddy. "You foolish woman. *Man.* 'Cause that's what you are. You think you can play around with heathen symbols, gather a—a coven of faggots—and escape the eye of the Lord? His will is mighty! He showed me this Coalrose creature is a demon."

"You're insane. They should have kept you at Bellevue," Isis said.

"For a month or more, the witch plagued my sleep, with images of black roses, roses that flew, and pricked and drew blood, like damned vampire bats. Then, the Lord showed me what had to be done. *'Thou shalt not suffer a witch to live.'* Exodus 22."

Still holding her close, he produced a lighter—a magic trick of his own.

"Let me inside," he said.

It was her choice to make. "Let everyone else go. I'm pretty sure that the Lord frowns on murder."

They were through the door and in the crowd. Someone, maybe Jasper, made the announcement to evacuate. Jeremiah pulled her to the side and watched as the club emptied. It was a stampede—the rumor of old crazy Jeremiad moved through the crowd quickly. Then, the sound of the piano rose above the mayhem. The melody was gentle, even soporific. It was "This Little Light of Mine" and "Lavender Green" and "When You Wish Upon a Star" and some other unknown melody, all woven together. The lullaby lulled the crowd, and the room emptied peacefully until there was just her, Jasper and the woman at the piano. And Jeremiah.

Jeremiah began flicking the lighter. It sparked. Soon, she would join the shadow folk, become ash and yellowed bones. Isis thought of Brother Creek, Mother Lightning, and Aunt Junebug. She heard her mother's harsh voice: "Isaiah, I told you this path would lead you straight to Hell." She thought of the goddess whose name she shared, and of the ankh, the symbol of life, the name of her club.

"Burn in hell, witch," said Jeremiah Black.

Zoë Coalrose gave no indication that she had heard him. She just kept on playing the piano, and the song evolved, gentle silvery notes tarnishing. Blackening, like the club was about to. The melody became harsher, atonal, the rhythm staccato. When she started singing, there were no words Isis recognized.

Jeremiah flicked the lighter again, and finally a teardrop of flame bloomed. It was not the only thing that bloomed.

Something dropped from the ceiling. It was black, curved like a clamshell, and it lazily drifted down and landed on Black's dripping suit. The tiny clamshell was blacker than the suit. Then another one fell. And another. These dark shapes spiraled down, all landing on Jeremiah. One of them doused the flame. Then, there were more, gently mantling his face, shoulders and shoes.

When the flame died, Isis knocked the lighter out of Jeremiah Black's hand. He hardly noticed. His face had gone as slack as Bucephalus Wilson's. The fight went out of Jeremiah. His rage deflated as he was buried in soft black petals.

Isis looked up to the ceiling and saw the rose vines encircling the pipes. The blooms were black as coal.

When Zoë played the last note of her wordless song, they vanished, like smoke.

Underglaze

The house was probably grand in its heyday, Maureen thought as she parked. It had a large front lawn of topiary that was so overgrown you couldn't tell what shapes they'd originally been. She could detect, just barely, the bulbous forms, like chess piece pawns and bishops, their silhouettes imprecise and sloppy. The house itself sprawled over a hill in a single level. It was painted yellow, though the paint was peeling, revealing the red brick skin beneath. Maureen passed a bird bath, streaked with old droppings and filled with black water. Only the printed sign that said Estate Sale taped on the door let her know that she was in the right place.

The door was unlocked. Stepping inside, Maureen felt like she had entered an alternate timeline, one in which the decor of the 1970s was still popular. The vinyl floor tile was bright orange and patterned with sunflowers. The light fixtures were molded plastic in organic-yet-mathematical shapes. And the furniture in the sunken living room had modular furniture in tones of avocado-green and harvest gold.

The house appeared to be empty.

She resisted the urge to announce herself. There probably wasn't anything she wanted here anyway. Her husband accused her of being addicted to estate sales. He might have been right. She couldn't resist them. There was an adrenaline spike that moved through her body every time she saw a sign for one. The thrill, though, was not in buying things. That was where Cyril was wrong (in spite of the many purchases she'd brought home). Maureen was addicted (if, indeed, it was an addiction) to exploring other people's houses. It was like walking into a person's memories. And the things she actually bought were messages from the dead to her. A vase, or chair, or painting wasn't just an object. It was a piece of the person's soul.

In the absence of any official, Maureen began to wander the house. The deceased woman collected odd things, that much was for sure. In one room, possibly a study, there was an antique roll top desk. The price, at $350, was pretty good, considering the excellent condition of the stained cherry wood. Maureen rolled up the ruffled desk covering.

She almost dropped her purse. A collection of yellowed bone skulls was concealed within. Bird skulls, mouse skulls, and the skull of some slightly larger creature, perhaps a cat or a ferret. The skulls themselves didn't bother her. She'd been in several boutique shops where animal bones and pinned butterflies were sold along with other tchotchkes like pocket watches or Limoges Boxes. She personally found such things macabre, but to each their own. What Maureen found disturbing was that someone had painstakingly placed objects in the eye sockets. The "eyes" were baubles of all colors. Little diamanté eyes of green, blue, pink, and yellow all gazed up at Maureen as if she had disturbed them. Maureen closed the desk, leaving the bone beasts to glitter on in darkness.

The next room she stepped into was filled with lamps that were also sculptures of African boys in turbans and balloon pants. The boys were all in servile poses and their painted "skin" was a shiny black that stood out against the bright white of their flowing outfits. Each of the black boy sculptures (there might have been twenty of them) grinned widely, their lips as red as blood. The lamps sat on the floor, on side and end tables, on an ottoman and a wall-length buffet. All of the bulbs in the lamps were on, and each bulb was a different color. "Party Lights," they were called at the home improvement store. Maureen saw pink, green, and blue light illuminating the blacker-than-black bric-a-brac. She even saw a couple of black-light bulbs. Black-light always nauseated her, and the purple glow on the fake black skin intensified that feeling. Maureen backed out of the room and closed the door for good measure.

The final room she entered was occupied by a thin, beaky-looking woman in a fluorescent green polyester blouse from the seventies, gray high-water pants, and penny loafers. Her brown and gray hair was styled like a mushroom cap. This woman flashed Maureen a toothy grin.

Maureen smiled back, even though she was uncomfortable. The woman's bespectacled gaze was intense. As she glanced away, something caught her eye.

There was an ugly curio cabinet in which three plates were vertically displayed. The plates looked like standard blue-and-white Willow-ware china, but the pattern was slightly blurred, and the blue was much, much richer. It was a beautiful blue that seemed to glow. It even bled onto the bone-white porcelain, staining it. The rims of the dishes were loops of blue that looked as if they could have been an elegant script she couldn't make out. The center of the plate had the portrait of a woman in an old-fashioned hoop skirt. She looked like a Southern belle in crinolines. Then the face changed.

Metamorphosed.

It became the face of a long-haired Persian cat with fur of spun cotton in an antebellum dress, like a feline Scarlett O'Hara. The blurry pattern changed again, right before her eyes. The figure in the dress had the face of an owl. Even in dark blue glaze, the eyes were wild and piercing.

Not unlike the owlish face of the woman with the mushroom cap hairdo.

"How much for the plates?" Maureen asked her.

The woman peered at her through her face-shielding bifocals. "The azure porcelain is quite lovely. They are quite rare," she said. Her voice was high and fluty. "The chemical compound for the transfer glaze is unknown. Legend has it that the glaze would stain the potter's hands. *Permanently.* How awful that would be: to have azure hands for the rest of your life. My word!"

"That sounds terrible," Maureen replied. "But how much?"

"Let me check the price list." The woman picked up a printout of old-style computer paper, the kind with perforations and striped green and white. Maureen noticed that the print was dot matrix. The whole house was trapped in a time warp.

Maureen waited for what seemed like an awkwardly long time as the woman peered at the printout. Behind the large spectacles, her eyes narrowed and widened as if they couldn't focus on the text in front of her. She gave an exasperated sigh and flung the printout down on a side table.

But when she looked at Maureen in the eye, her face settled into a semblance of calm, and she smiled. Her teeth were tombstone white.

"Mrs. Ingrid LeFevre was my mother," said Mushroom Cap. "Momma was, to be frank, quite eccentric."

Maureen nodded, even though she had no idea of where this conversation was going.

Mushroom Cap continued. "It could be very exasperating."

Maureen made a noncommittal sound in response.

"She had certain, how shall we say, queer notions about some of her objects."

"I see," Maureen said. "If you'll excuse me . . ."

"No, I fear you don't understand."

"Pardon?"

"Momma believed that certain possessions should, upon the occasion of her death, be bequeathed to deserving persons."

"I don't know what that means? Three-hundred is my limit."

"Oh dear," said the woman, who was quickly getting on her nerves. "What I mean to say is this: Momma wants—or wanted—me to ask you a question about the plates before the estate should part with them."

"What's the question?" Maureen knew she sounded short, but her patience was wearing thin.

"The question is simple. What faces did you see in the Azure Porcelain plates—the three that are displayed?"

"That's it?" Maureen glanced at the plates in the cabinet. And found that she was somewhat speechless. What she saw was amazingly nonsensical, but to speak it aloud would be madness.

She spoke, nevertheless. "The plate on the right has the face of a goat. There are hooves sticking out of the sleeves. The face in the middle is some kind of anthropomorphic root vegetable. I think it's a turnip—isn't it clever how the stalks are arranged like hair? And the last plate, I see a squid. It has a friendly face as far as squids go. I guess."

"How splendid," said Mushroom Cap. "You may take the plates."

Maureen fumbled in her purse for her wallet.

"My dear woman," LeFevre's daughter said. For some reason, Maureen thought she looked like a Hortense or a Mildred. She had the look of someone who would have an ugly, old-timey name redolent of floral perfume, tart lemonade, and licorice. "There is no reason, whatsoever to pay. Ingrid wished this sui generis set of azure porcelain find a home with 'a kindred spirit.'"

"Did she now?"

"Indeed. I shall wrap them up for you. Momma would be happy knowing that they have found a new home."

Maureen didn't respond to that as she hefted the box up. What was there to say?

Cyril was singing in the kitchen when she got home. Singing and cooking. Maureen saw raw flank steak, a colander full of fresh spinach and a bowl of quartered red bliss potatoes. Cyril didn't hear her coming because he was listening to music on his headphones and pulsing the food processor. The counter was full of tiny messes, including discarded basil stems and papery garlic skins. She also noticed a pink bakery box on the table. She placed the box with the plates next to it.

"You got the job," Maureen said after Cyril had taken off his earphones and kissed her hello.

"I start next Monday," he said, beaming. "I even get a corner office. With a good view!"

"So, you thought you'd celebrate," she said. She smiled at her husband. "Let me guess: steak with chimichurri sauce, garlic mashed potatoes, and red velvet cake."

"Close but no cigar," Cyril said and swatted her on her butt. "That's not a red velvet cake in that box. It's—" He stopped, noticing her own box. "What's that?"

"Something I picked up from an estate sale," she said.

"Lord," he said. "You and your garage sales."

"It was an *estate* sale," she said, "and you won't believe what I found. And you really won't believe the price." She opened the box and began removing the plates, which were all swaddled in newspaper and bubble wrap. She removed the wrapping from three plates, setting them down. The hue was intense against the white kitchen table. "Aren't they gorgeous?"

Cyril silently hovered over the three dishes. The woman in the dress in these plates had the head of a lioness, an antelope, and a heron. The faces slowly changed. The optical illusion was amazing. "They sure are *something*," he finally said.

"You don't like them?"

"Well," he said.

"Well, what?"

"Well, they are odd. Are they supposed to be antique or something? The faces look like those inkblots that shrinks use. Someone must have screwed up at the China factory."

Maureen looked at the three plates that lay on the white table.

"You don't see her?" Maureen said.

"See who, honey? All I see are a bunch of Jackson Pollack paint splatters where a head ought to be. The color's nice, though. How much did they cost?"

"They were free," Maureen said. The big reveal, though, was anti-climactic. To her, at least. She was disturbed by the fact that her husband, and apparently, Mildred/Hortense, couldn't see the ever-changing faces in the ceramics.

Cyril said, "That's good news. I can't imagine that they were worth much."

"You hate them."

"Oh, now honey. They're not to my taste. But what do I know? I would be happy filling the house with pictures of dogs playing poker."

She unwrapped another dish of the set. This time, the azure lady had the face of a weasel. The weasel's eyes were soft, the whiskers so expertly rendered Maureen could imagine the whisper-tickle against her skin.

"I've got to finish up dinner. Maureen, would you mind setting the table?"

She pulled out another dish. This time, the azure lady had the head of a bear. A great grizzly, with massive paws poking through the dress sleeves. The bear seemed to be smiling at her, beneath the glaze.

"Maureen? Honey? Did you hear me?"

She put the plate down, gently. "I heard you. Should we have a Cabernet or a Malbec?"

Every now and then, Maureen suffered bouts of insomnia. It wasn't often enough to warrant a prescription. She could make do with over-the-counter sleep aids. The problem was, she usually diagnosed her insomnia in the small hours of the morning. Any medication she took now would keep her groggy well into the next day.

Oh well. She'd drink lots of coffee at work and maybe leave early. Right now, she was wide awake. There wasn't a hint of exhaustion anywhere. She was wired, just as if she'd had several espressos. She heard Cyril lightly snoring next to her. In the half-light, she could see his relaxed face, his mouth slightly open.

When she got bored of looking at his child-like slumber and the cracks on the ceiling, she sat up and got out of bed. After gathering her robe and her tablet, she left the bedroom and headed downstairs. She planned to read in the living room.

But Maureen found she couldn't really concentrate on the words on the small screen. She couldn't absorb them. The book club had picked this novel, titled Caw, because it was short and had won a major literary award. But it was densely written and confusing. Every labyrinthine sentence had multiple meanings. Even the character names were symbolic. Or maybe they weren't; it just seemed awfully on-the-nose to name a clashing married couple Cyan (the male) and Ruby. The author was fond of repeating images, or motifs. Seagulls showed up with alarming regularity, and at one point both Ruby and Cyan believed it was the same seagull, who may or may not have been the ghost of their dead drowned child. Dreary sea imagery popped up. Green waves, gold waves, white foam, spume, clumps of algae. The grey sea, the azure sea. It was the sort of novel that Mildred or Ingrid might enjoy, Maureen decided. Caw was grotesque and impenetrable.

Maureen turned off her tablet. She found herself drifting toward the kitchen. She was through the double doors and at the table and began unpacking the dishes. She saw a vixen, a wolf, and a raven. The twelfth and final plate had the head of a seagull. It was a very Beatrix Potter-like seagull. She even wore a dainty hat. Each of the creatures had warm, soulful eyes. In fact, they had the same eyes. Whereas the ornate gown and the fur and vegetable matter had all been rendered in exquisite detail, the eyes were all simple. They were just pure circles. Blue orbs, like marbles. A child could have drawn them. And yet, they seemed to be alive.

Maureen shuddered. She remembered the diamanté eyes of the skulls in Ingrid LeFevre's house. And how the eyes of those turbaned black boy lamps stared at her. She shrugged the queer feeling off and stacked the plates. She lifted the box, intending to break it down for recycling. It was heavy; more than just discarded bubble wrap was in that box. Maureen dug through the trash until she reached the bottom and unearthed the thirteenth plate.

Like the others, it was the same rich azure color and featured the ornate, ruffled, and lace-adorned gown. But it was missing a face. Where a face should have been, Maureen saw a storm cloud of chaos. It was an azure inkblot, just like her husband had said all of the dishes were. A wild and careless mistake that stood out in stark relief against the delicately etched dress. The "hands" were also explosions of blue, a child's drawing of a bomb going off.

This plate, like all of the others in the set, had a filigree decoration around the rim, a series of fine swirls that mimicked elegant script but was essentially nonsense. But on this plate, it seemed to spell out something. She couldn't make it out, but she was sure that there was a message in those azure letters.

Maureen decided that this plate, with the faceless woman, was her favorite. She couldn't say why. She turned the kitchen light on to examine the plate more.

The formless mass where the face should have been was, somehow, an even more intense color. If it were a pool, she would swim in its depths. Even the clearest cloudless sky couldn't compete with this blue. She could have stared at it for hours. It was so beautiful.

Maureen found herself in the fridge, taking out the bourbon pecan tart. She cut a slice of the pie and put it on the azure plate.

The change was immediate and inexorable. The slice turned blue. Crust, the gelled syrup filling, the pecans. It was bright, glowingly so. Maureen paused. She should really wake her husband, if only to share this miraculous, supernatural moment with him. But Cyril slept like the dead and woke up evil. Besides, didn't he say he couldn't see the designs in the dish sets? Maybe he couldn't see this slice of sea and sky.

She took up her fork. Paused, thinking of paint-based poisons. But only for a moment. She devoured the pie. It tasted of a hidden grotto where the shrine to a forgotten sea goddess sits with offerings of flowers—candles flickering and water lambent. It tasted of a sky where no cloud ever floated or bird ever flew, just a flawless expanse of blue. It also tasted of bourbon, butter, and pecan.

The slice of azure was gone, wolfed down. She lifted the thirteenth plate, intending to wash it. She saw crumbs of blue pastry on the surface. Before she could get to the sink, they were absorbed by the faceless blue face. She saw the specks go under the glaze and into the blue void. Then they disintegrated.

Cyril was up and out of the house before she woke up. There was a hastily scrawled note about a 6 A.M. conference call with clients in Shanghai.

"You must of had some kinda dream," he wrote. Maureen twitched; Cyril was always saying (and writing) "must of" instead of "must have." It was a pet peeve of hers.

Maureen had gotten to back to bed after her midnight snack. She fell asleep shortly after that. The dreams, which she remembered in scraps, were vivid and quite wonderful. Maureen was on a boat made of porcelain, on a turbulent sea. At various points, she was visited by the jewel-encrusted bones of sea creatures. She recalled a giant squid made of opals with chocolate diamonds for its eyes and beak.

She felt well rested and clearheaded. But apparently, she'd done something in her sleep to disturb Cyril, which was odd. Cyril had slept though thunderstorms with hailstones that sounded like castanets on the roof. He'd even slept through a mild earthquake that had managed to destroy a fair amount of the glass figurines she'd been collecting.

Maureen shrugged it off, making a note to text him about it later that day.

"I really like that scarf," said the barista as she foamed the milk for Maureen's morning latte. She had a pixie cut that was dyed bright pink, and her ears had hoops marching up and down her lobes.

"Oh, thanks," Maureen replied absently. She was slightly embarrassed that she'd been caught staring at the girl, whose arms were also heavily tattooed sleeves. The tattooed arms were a busy swirl of color, but Maureen saw shapes in them. On the right arm, there was a cat's face, an owl's head, a goat, a bear, and a lioness. On the right, she saw a fox, a wolf, and a seagull.

"Where did you get it?" the barista asked. Her name tag identified her as *Jinwen*.

"This? It was a gift from my mother-in-law." Maureen reflexively touched the cheaply made scarf looped around her neck at the last minute before leaving the house.

And gasped.

The scarf that Aimee, Cyril's mother, had given her years ago, had been a washed-out, pale, powder blue, prosaic and ordinary. It had probably been bought on sale at a dollar store. The scarf Maureen now wore was azure heading into sapphire. It was a piece of the sea wrapped around her throat. It almost hurt to look at.

It was the same color as the plates.

"Ma'am? Your drink is ready." Some impatient douchebag in a Panama hat looked up from his iPhone, gave her the "hurry up" gesture. Maureen looked from the blindingly blue scarf to see that her latte was perched on the counter. She took her drink.

Jinwen's foam-art was one of the many reasons this coffee shop had a loyal clientele. She crafted steamed milk into hearts, tulips, and Hello Kitty. The white cloud of foam was sculpted into the shape of a woman's profile, her hair up in a fancy chignon. But there was no face. There was a void with a trail of bubbles trailing out from the empty gaze.

It was through sheer force of will that Maureen did not drop the cup. She carefully walked over to the sugar and cream station and set her cup down. She took her phone out, snapped a picture before dropping in sugar packets, which destroyed the image.

"I am not going insane," she said aloud on the walk to her parked car. There was no one else there, and she wouldn't have cared even if there were. She vocalized her thoughts all the time. It helped her focus.

She got in her car and sat down. Took a few sips of her latte.

She took out her phone and opened her browser.

"Azure Porcelain" was the first thing she typed. She clicked the first link and read:

'Azure Porcelain' was a brand of novelty ceramics made by LeFevre & Co from 1900–1920. It was a parody of the popular Flo-Blue (or Flown Blue) style of dinnerware. The scenes on the dishes were often whimsical with references to (then) contemporary doggerel and drinking songs. They were discontinued due to poor sales and not, as rumor had it, due to the

toxicity of the chemical glaze. The story, that the glaze was derived from a strong cyanotoxic algae, however, encouraged the collectability of intact sets.

"Ok," Maureen said aloud. At least this wiki was convinced that the idea that the azure dishes somehow *stained* their owners as ridiculous. Because of course that was ridiculous. Mildred/Hortense with the mushroom cap hairstyle was crazy. But there was still the fact of the luminous azure scarf. And the faceless woman in her foam art.

Maureen asked her phone, "Search for Ingrid LeFevre."

The first and second hits directed to LeFevre & Co. The third link was productive, being a history of the LeFevre family. She scrolled past the bios of company founder Arvid LeFevre and his brother Osvald until she found what she was looking for.

Ingrid LeFevre was pictured, an old-timey photographic portrait that had a slight plum-colored hue to it. She was a white woman with wide eyes, a heart-shaped face with her ringleted hair fashioned into bun on top of her head.

"You've got to be kidding me," Maureen muttered.

The dress Ingrid wore was an exact replica of the ornate gown that the many-faced lady wore on those plates.

"Where did you get that lipstick, girl?" asked Diane, one of the secretaries, when she walked into the office.

"I love those shoes," said Justin, one of her fellow instructors.

She passed an obstacle course of admiration before she made it into the ladies' room. She stood in front of the mirror, shocked and unsurprised at the same time.

Maureen was covered in azure. Everything was beautifully and terrifyingly blue. Bright, electric blue. The simple black tunic dress she'd thrown on was blue. As blue as the scarf around her neck. And her shoes. And her makeup, both lipstick and eyeshadow.

"I look like a damn Smurf," she said to her reflection. Or that little girl in the Willie Wonka movie who turned into a blueberry.

Even so, Maureen had to admit, she looked good. Azure was her color. It played nicely against her dark skin.

She reached up to flake off some of the eyeshadow. It was a little too thickly applied; she'd been running late. A piece of it chipped off. It had an oddly *solid* texture. The chip hit the bathroom counter. And shattered, like a piece of pottery. Maureen felt a tickle at the spot where the flake of eyeshadow had been. It was a pinprick, small but insistent. She ignored it, and focused on the piece of eyeshadow on the counter. It was jagged and crystalline in structure. She touched it.

"Ouch!"

It stabbed her finger before turning into powder. She put her finger into her mouth and slowly backed away from the mirror.

Maureen didn't have to teach any classes that day. She just had office hours, during which no student visited save during finals. She closed the door to the room and continued searching on the internet for Ingrid LeFevre.

She found a death notice from a month ago:

INGRID LEFEVRE (March 30, 1926–April 9, 2017). Heiress to the LeFevre company. Socialite, trailblazer, patron of the arts, collector of oddities. Survived by her daughter Harriet Ohm. In lieu of flowers, please donate to the LeFevre Foundation.

"Collector of oddities." The phrase caused her spine to tingle with disgust. She saw the silent stares of black lamp boys and the glittering eyes of the skulls. She no longer liked the plates. They were no longer whimsical.

"Harriet Ohm?"

"Speaking." Maureen immediately recognized the fluty voice.

"Hello. This is Maureen Sexton. We met yesterday. At the estate sale on Sunday?"

"Are you scheduling a delivery? Let me get the number of the moving company—"

"No. I'm not having anything delivered. You gave me the dinnerware? The Azure Porcelain?"

"Oh, yes! I remember you. Quite the lucky girl, you are! You know, they are collector's items . . ."

Maureen bristled at being called *girl*. She let it slide, though. There were more important things to contend with at the moment. More of her eyeshadow had crumbled off. Chips of azure pottery littered her work desk. "Was your mother the model for the lady in the dress?"

"Why, yes. She was quite the *belle de jour!* Her father thought it would be a scream to have her immortalized in ceramic."

"I . . . thank you. Thank you very much," said Maureen. She hung up the phone; she knew what she had to do.

Immortalized in ceramic.

Even now, her bones made a hollow scraping sound, like the tines of a fork against fine china.

By the time she got home, the lines in Maureen's hand were blue, like veins of lapis lazuli. The glazed fingernails on her left hand were fissured, like the surface of an antique vase.

Maureen stumbled into the kitchen where the plates were. The color was no longer intense. The design was washed out, the color of faded blue jeans. All plates were ghosts of what they had been. All, save one.

The faceless woman was no longer sitting in her circle. She stood, facing Maureen. The void where her face should have been was an undulating, turbulent oval of lovely blue. It was both an eye and a mouth. The nonsense script encircling the rim of the plate burned azure.

Without a moment's hesitation, Maureen picked up the plate and smashed it on the floor.

Mirror Bias

Silver atoms danced as light hit the plane. It diffused, refracted, re-formed on the panes. Images shaped from light and dark and vivid color. Captured in reverse: the man in room of flowers. He walked among the green-blue bombs of hydrangeas, the slender necks of lilies, the misshapen hands and hearts of orchid petals. Bouquets of roses in a variety of colors, pink, yellow, white, and yes, red, sat in glass-paneled refrigerators. He tended to sprigs of white baby's breath, sprays of yellow chrysanthemums, bunches of larkspur, amaryllis, iris, and carnations.

The day started off terribly. First, the order of poinsettias was substandard. The leaves were a wan pink, as if they'd been drained of vitality. Then, the Verifone machine stopped working, so Percy had to use a phone application to process credit payments. Then a high-maintenance customer in an ivory power suit, black slingbacks and a Coach purse complained about the available selection: the bleached poinsettias, and the lack of gladiolas, carnations, and peonies. It was all he could do not to tell the Devil Wears Prada wannabe off. (*You ain't Miss Daisy, and I ain't your butler, Miss Karen*). By the time the afternoon lull occurred, Percy was tense. He needed a cigarette, but he had quit years ago. He sat down for what seemed like the first time that day, and considered closing up shop. Foot traffic was minimal, and most of Chloris's business was conducted over the phone or the Internet.

Instead, he checked his phone. There were no messages but there was one notification from a dating app called Mirror-Bias. Percy clicked on it, only mildly curious. He hadn't had any luck on any of the apps. Everyone wanted manly men with porn star bodies and that just wasn't Percy. He was a florist, perhaps the gayest of all professions. And he was hardly in the best of shape. The middle-aged spread had started, and the hair on his head was developing the same horseshoe-patterned bald spot as his dad. But some stubborn streak of libido lingered, and he kept the apps on his phone.

<I know that you don't think so, but you are as beautiful as the flowers you sell.>

The words floated in a translucent blue bubble the color of a cleaning product on his phone screen. He immediately clicked to the page of the profile user. It was just a black screen, and with no user name. He clicked back to the message screen, and typed.

<Thank you. I think . . . 😊. Who are you?>

A pop sounded, indicating that a new message had arrived.

<Just someone who admires you from afar. I have for some time.>

Percy looked up from his phone, glancing outside. Chloris was on a side street, next to a beauty shop and Yoga studio, and across the street from a high-end pharmacy, a liquor store and a Peruvian restaurant. Mrs. Perreria ran Curl and Set and had an all-female staff. A hippie chick named Indiana ran the Yoga Studio, and while there were occasional male instructors, Namaste was primarily geared toward millennial women. The sleek, industrial-looking Caduceus Medicine never seemed to be occupied.

He typed: <Do you have any pictures?>

A few of them came through. They were all pictures of Percy in the shop. There was a shot of him tending the lilies, another misting some orchids. A picture of him talking to a customer as he wrapped up roses in florist's paper, and another of him arranging an assortment of flowers in a vase.

Percy put the phone down, his hands shaking. When and where had someone taken those pictures? They were close-up and in high definition.

Just then, the door to shop opened. A middle-aged white man in a Brooks Brothers suit with salt-and-pepper hair, owlish glasses, and a slight overbite entered.

"Sorry to startle you," he said, his voice slightly flavored by a twang. "I was wondering if you have any roses. It's my wife's birthday . . ."

After the transaction finished and Percy was alone once again, he looked at the message.

He typed: <1. That is creepy. Should I get a restraining order? 2. I meant, do you have any pictures of *yourself*?>

Percy regretted hitting send on the message, because he knew that the smart thing to do would be to enable the 'block' feature on the app. But his curiosity got the better of him. He thought, what killed the cat?

The pop of a message: <Percy, I have no wish to alarm you! I just have no ˌmojo' to this method of communication. I find it awkward. As to your second question, I will send pictures shortly, but please, examine my profile picture again.>

The profile was still blank. Just a square of blackness. Or was there just the slightest hint of blue? Percy stared at the screen, and gradually, pixel by pixel, an image came into shape. It was a face, or at least, part of one. The lighting was dim, almost non-existent. He saw an eye, half of a nose, lips. The skin seemed to be blacker than the blackness around it. It was all monochrome, save for the eye. It was blue.

But no ordinary blue. It cycled through the whole spectrum of blue with a strobe light effect. It was the blue of sapphires, or heliotropes. The blue of Prussia and Persia. The blue of cobalt and cornflowers. Violet-blue and blue dusk. All of these.

Percy supposed that there was some photo application he didn't know about, but the effect was amazing. He heard the sound of incoming messages. His nameless stalker had sent five images. At first, he thought they were in black and white, but they weren't. It was the subjects of the camera images that were so dark. One image was the close-up of a torso. The skin was smooth dark, the nipples even darker, like voids. It looked like a statue made of onyx. Percy zoomed on the image. There were no pores, pimples, skin tags, discolorations, or anything at all. Just perfection.

Percy's own body was full of all those flaws. He had lightning-like stretch marks, an ugly pink puckered scar from when he'd had gallbladder surgery.

The next picture was of a dick, big and black. It was erect, uncut and full of raised veins bulging just beneath the skin.

Percy's own penis was relatively small, something that always disappointed the tricks he'd had in the past. It was a sad little thing, more like a plant bulb than a phallus. This, and his lowkey effeminacy, always made him take the passive, bottom role sexually, something he didn't particularly enjoy.

Another picture was a close-up of the eyes. That strange, strobing effect was still active. The intensity of the blue irises emphasized the surreal darkness of the skin around it.

Percy's own eyes were deep-set, watery-brown, hidden behind thick lenses to correct an astigmatism.

As he flipped through the pictures, he realized that this statuesque man was his physical opposite. Percy also knew that the person sending the messages probably looked nothing like those images. He was probably a middle-aged loser like himself, struggling with weight problems.

He shut the app off, disgusted with his neediness. Percy knew he was being Catfished. It was a sick mental game people played, sometimes over years. The Catfisher preyed on the Catfishee's desperation, and exploited it for fun and profit.

He spent the rest of the day going over the finances. It was dark by the time he closed up the shop. Daylight saving time had just started, and the lamps had begun to ignite at 5 P.M.. Winter-dark seemed more intense than any other kind. It was more black than blue, and starlight was, somehow, weaker. He turned the light off.

The shop was cast in darkness. All of the glass surfaces became reflective. In the industrial garden box, the man paused, as if he sensed something. Did he feel eyes of sapphire blue on him? Perhaps. Did he tremble with a sudden chill? The man looked in the various reflections. The sheer pane of the front shop window, the backlit ultraviolet glow of the refrigerator, where the lilies lived. He found nothing. Only his own reflection, ghost-transparent. He walked out of the darkened shop, and locked up.

Dinner was a chicken salad sandwich he picked up from the supermarket deli and a glass of red wine. The chicken salad was chunky, lightly dressed with mayonnaise and had chunks of seedless green grapes. The sandwich bread was thick-cut, black, and slightly sweet. The Pinot Noir was crisp and acidic. Percy always had a glass with dinner. His doctor told him that one glass of wine was healthy for his heart, and besides, it helped him relax.

He felt the wine course through his bloodstream. It warmed him, and he felt the fuzzy drone of gentle inebriation. The television was on, a rerun of a '90s show starring the comedian Monique that Percy knew was stupid, but he enjoyed it anyway. As Monique and her stupid daughter chattered and exchanged catchphrases in the background, Percy brought out his phone, woke it up. He bypassed email and social media apps, and went straight for Mirror-Bias.

The interface for the app was a thing of beauty. Percy was closer to Luddite than technophile, but the graphics of the platform hit all of his aesthetic sweet spots. Mirror-Bias was sleek, clean, and minimalist, like one of those modern buildings downtown that captured the sky in steel slices. The font was all sans serif and in Art Deco-styled capitals. The radial buttons were elegant shell-like cornices. The profiles were encased in silvery gridlines.

He had a message. <You are the rarest flower of them all.> There was a link pasted into the message. Against his better judgment, Percy activated the hyperlink. It led to his shop's website, Chloris.com. All of his featured floral designs were represented, but each of them had been recast with the darkest of blooms.

The "Thinking of You" vase was filled with pansies a deep red-black, and the vase itself was transparent and black. "Sorry for Your Loss" had dark purple tulips and sprigs of gray baby's breath. The wedding collection had table arrangements of macabre-looking black dahlias peeking up through waxy ivy leaves.

Percy said, "What the hell is this?"

Mirror-Bias pinged with the arrival of a new message. <It is what I see when I look at your work. You are so talented, Percival.>

<Thank you> he typed back. Percy was confused. Surely it was a coincidence that his blue-eyed, black-skinned stalker had texted an answer to his spoken rhetorical question? Nevertheless, Percy shivered. This person was playing games, and it was as creepy as hell.

"Who are you?" Percy said aloud. He got ready to type out the words, rephrased as "let's talk on the phone" when a response bubble appeared.

<I told you. I just admire you and your work every day. I am no-one special.>

"Do you have a name?" Percy said. He must be hallucinating, or maybe the app had somehow accessed his phone. The technology was always evolving. The very idea of video calls, like Skype, had been science fiction when he'd been a child. Maybe this weirdo had somehow hacked Mirror-Bias.

The ill-advised hyperlink he'd activated was probably the culprit. Disgusted, Percy turned off his phone.

The blue-black screen of death flared. Then the iPhone screen became a black mirror. A reflecting void.

Percy was maybe five minutes into his pre-bedtime shower when he noticed that the steam produced by the jet of hot water was unusually thick. His building's water heater was notoriously overtaxed and in winter, tepid water was the expected norm. A dense billowing wall of steam now filled his bathroom. He couldn't see the commode, the sink or the wall-length mirror through its wavering, curling tendrils.

He had a momentary panic that there was a fire and he was trapped. That quickly passed. It was too thin and vaporous to be smoke. Percy stayed under the shower for a couple more minutes. When he turned the water off, he saw that the steam hadn't dissipated. If anything, it was thicker, and seemed to have a fibrous quality, like airborne cotton.

Percy toweled off in the shower, which was a stall encased in glass. It was like a cage, or a coffin. It kept the heat in an otherwise chilly bathroom. He stayed inside, mesmerized by the swirling mist. It seemed to be moving, in ripples, eddying around invisible stones. It was like the visualized breath of the north wind seen in old European maps.

He watched as the substance shifted and shaped itself.

Percy gasped. He was awestruck by what he saw. His soul was shredded to ribbons by sheer terror and wonder. The steam rearranged itself into familiar, comforting shapes.

He saw bell-shaped tulips, the long skirts of lilies, the alien headdresses of orchids, the elegant whorls of roses. It was as if Chloris had been recreated in his bathroom, out of the filigree tracery of steam. The pearly grey phantom flowers were ephemeral. Their edges were wispy, their outlines shimmering, like heat mirages, threatening to come apart.

"Well, shit," Percy said aloud. It was finally happening, He was going insane. His aunt Elaine had begun seeing hallucinations around his age. He'd been a child then. He recalled a moment when Elaine had been visiting his parents' house, and she claimed, at breakfast, that she saw the face of her guardian angel in her cereal milk. She had described the angel's face in such vivid detail that young Percy stood beside her and searched for Sapphira (the angel's name). Later in the year, Elaine was committed for treatment. Percy was sad, but not for Elaine's illness. He was sad that the world was such a cruel place, where angelic sightings were signs of insanity.

The garden of steam flowers before him now was more elaborate than an angel's face in a bowl of milk and soggy bran flakes could ever be.

Percy stared at the blooms of condensation for a minute more. Then he pressed against the stall door.

That's when he saw the figure in the mist. It was more of a dim suggestion, vaguely shaped like a torso. It was dark, the torso, ink-black. The sheer blackness of the torso cut through the thick fog. It was a radiant darkness. The figure stood maybe five feet away, which was impossible, because that would mean that the figure was behind the mirror.

No. It meant that the figure was in the mirror itself.

"Sweet Jesus," Percy murmured. He moved away from the stall door, and huddled in the triangular wedge beneath the dormant shower head. It was the right move, because the torso began to walk. It stepped out of the mirror, and over the sink.

It.

Not it; he. Thick legs like the trunk of a tree, thick arms roped with vine-like veins. He walked through the field of mist-flowers, right up to the shower stall. A hairless, musclebound golem with eyes of piercing blue.

(Sapphire blue).

He was more like a statue than a man.

"Who are you?" Percy said.

The figure stood silently. Then, with rapid grace, opened the door to the stall. It, pushed Percy down to the level of its genitals. The monstrous penis and balls were black and reflective, like the highly waxed exterior of a funeral hearse.

Percy knew what to do, but there was no way he could accommodate the shiny genitalia. It was so sculptural and shiny, it was unerotic. But his lips unwrapped the heavy glans, nonetheless. He didn't taste flesh, though. It was too smooth and poreless for that. It was cool and metallic in his mouth. He saw the distorted reflection of his face as he blew the statue being.

He was handsome, even, hot, in that concave/convex mirror image. He didn't have on his unflattering glasses, so the rich brown of his eyes was obvious. His skin was luminous, smooth and golden in the black mirrored skin of the being.

Percy found himself getting hard. He opened his mouth wide, until the mirror-cock was deep in his throat. He massaged it with his tongue and throat muscles.

When the statue being came, it withdrew its penis from Percy's mouth. Glittery black liquid spurted from the urethra and landed on Percy's face and chest. It stung. The semen was made of tiny shards of glass that ground themselves into Percy's skin. It was painful, but he didn't care. The cuts opened tiny mouths on his skin, eager for more laceration.

The being spurted one more crystal-black arc. The steam flowers came apart. And so did the mirror being.

Into a million reflecting fragments.

EIDOLON REALTY, LLC.

PRIVATE PLACEMENT MEMORANDUM (Confidential)

SLIDE 1: Eidolon Realty is the only firm that specializes in the procurement and maintenance of properties with paranormal activity.

Image: The Eidolon Realty logo, all capital art nouveau font from the '40s dark grey with dandelion-yellow shadowing that has a 3D effect.

We have properties all over the globe in addition to the U.S. We have a strong presence in Latin America, particularly Peru and Argentina. ER has property in Asia (Laos, Vietnam, and Hong Kong), Central Europe (Georgia, Ukraine, the Czech Republic) and is in the process of acquiring properties in Nigeria and Eritrea.

SLIDES 2 - 7:
•A house made of woven reeds overlooking a silvery lake.
•A stone house on a cloud-covered mountaintop with a llama chomping on grass.
•A skyscraper rising above a miasma of brown-grey haze.
•A snow-dappled dacha, blue-gray mountains in the distance.
•A wooden box of a house on stilts, rising above claylike earth.
•A dwelling that looks like a thatched beehive that sits in the midst of a lush green savannah.

How did Eidolon Realty start, and where did we get our first property? It started back in 1992, with our founder Hamish Truxton.

SLIDE 8: Image: Mr. Truxton, age 21. A tall, thin Caucasian with shoulder-length auburn hair in a tie-dyed T-shirt that says PHISH, cargo shorts, and well-worn out sandals.

Truxton graduated from Harvey Mudd with a degree in biostatistics in 1992. That summer he took a vacation in Scotland, and rented a cottage on Wyre off the coast in the Orkneys, "to get away from it all." Wyre is sparsely populated, if you don't count the grey seals that nest there.

SLIDE 9: Image: The cottage. Made of slate and shale, with a roof of black bitumen. Moss grows in the mortar, making the whole lopsided cottage look like a loaf of moldy bread.

SLIDE 10: Image: Cottage interior. A single room, lacquered wooden floor, iron bed frame with lumpy mattress, small fridge and oven, a door that leads to a bathroom, presumably.

SLIDE 11: Video of Truxton, in the present day. More professional short hair style, hair faded to brown, glasses, suit, and tie.
"The cottage dated from the late 1800s, and save for the modern conveniences, was mostly unchanged. It sat on a grassy knoll, and from one side you could see the North Sea. It was about a mile away from any other habitation, perfect for isolation, which is what I wanted. I saw more seals than I did people. But soon, I realized that I wasn't alone."

SLIDE 12: Image: The image of a woman. It is an old-timey sepia photo with ragged edges. The woman has a beak-like nose, which is accentuated by her severe hairdo—black hair frosted with gray gathered in a kind of chignon. Black eyes glare from over the impressive nose. Piercing eyes. Eyes that don't smile, but eyes that frown and judge everything you do. This thin, avian face sits on a long stalk of a neck that rises from the lace-trimmed collar of a black blouse.
Truxton voice resumes: "The cottage was the summer residence of one Shulamith Liebling, a German Expressionist painter who moved to Glasgow during the ascent of the Third Reich. She is most famous for depictions of nascent fascism done in bistre tones, featuring woodland animals. Her most famous painting is 'Konig Dachs,' which features a demonic-looking badger threatening a nest of childishly drawn moles. She used the cottage on Wyre as a studio from late 1940s until her death in 1968. Liebling kept to herself, going to the village only for groceries and cigarettes. She would wander around the island in her black dresses, puffing away, during

the frequent fogs (the Haar, it's called in Scotland). Local children thought that she was the Morrigan."

SLIDE 13: Image: A color photograph of the inside of the cottage. By the blackened fireplace, there is a section of the film that looks blurred. The blurred section is roughly shaped like a ball of light, greenish in tint. The blurry ball is transparent, like green cellophane. The edges of the ball are rough, as if it were a tear, and not some filmic anomaly.

"Ms. Liebling began manifesting the third night of my stay. At first, she was subtle. She would only appear when my back was turned, for instance. I would get the feeling that someone—something—was looking at me, and I'd turn, and only catch a fading wisp of green mist. Of course, I thought I was going insane."

SLIDE 14: Image: A photo of a column of mist, roughly the height of a woman. Through granular verdigris tones, there is a suggestion of a dress, a long thin neck, and, on top of the green smoke, a head. The features are indistinct, but you can make out two holes where eyes should be, a gash for a mouth filled with blackened gums and rotted fangs. She had no nose or hair. The head alone is haloed in vivid green flames.

Truxton's voice: "Needless to say, when Shulamith Liebling manifested in this form, I took the picture, and left that night. For a long time, a decade or so, I did not tell anyone about my experience. I knew nobody would believe me anyway. Later, I learned that Liebling had killed herself in the very same cottage, with a mixture of strychnine and morphine. She was discovered by the maid who kept the place clean, her body twisted, her face frozen with the tormented grin that her ghostly visage revealed.

"The idea for Eidolon Realty came from a visit in Ukraine. I had visited a seed fund in Kiev, and I took a couple of days afterwards and stayed at a dacha in the nearby countryside. It turns out that it, too, was haunted."

SLIDE 15: Image: A tin-roofed, one-story wooden house with a large circular front window. The wood structure is painted Prussian blue and surrounded by pines.

SLIDE 16: Image: The darkened interior of the dacha. Ceramics—patterned plates and pewter mugs—surround the walls' high shelves. A samovar sits on a round table with bone china laid out. A cloud hovers by a squat wooden stove. The wan and waxen face of a youth appears in the center of this cloud, and seeping wounds the color of spiderwebs appear on his beautiful face. Though stripped of color, it is obvious that in life his hair was blond and his eyes clear blue.

Narration: "Pytr Ivanovich, age 23. The dacha had been in his family for years, and he spent many a summer there as a child. During his late teens, Pytr hung with a rough crowd and became hooked on Krokodil, which was the eventual cause of his demise.

"Ivanovich was a violent poltergeist. He shattered half of the crockery you see in the room. They would detonate, hand grenades made of porcelain. My companion at the time was my girlfriend. Far from being terrified or disquieted, she was beyond thrilled to witness the paranormal in action. When I told Martha about the Liebling haunting in Scotland, she'd insisted that we visit that property.

"It was she who first came up with the idea of Eidolon Realty."

SLIDE 17: Eidolon Realty offers three subsidiary paranormal properties.

•Spectral Properties feature ghosts that are locked in loops. These souls are unaware that they are ghosts and cannot affect their physical environment.

•The Phantasm Estates brand specializes in more interactive apparitions. These spirits talk and shape shift, much like Shulamith Liebling. While they can don more sinister aspects, they are by and large, harmless.

•Eidolon Realty's assets are full on poltergeists. These assets are mostly purchased by researchers and movie studios.

SLIDES 18 - 20: Financial charts and data supplied by Bloomberg.

(K)naivety

The spangletrees on the isle of Shaangö don't have leaves. The branches are stark and bare. But at dusk, in the crepuscular light, they issue a mist that shrouds everything in sparkling webs. The vaporous webs grow and glisten, full of metallic dust. The glittering dust settles and slowly vanishes, and by the next morning, it dissipates, burned off by the sun. No-one knows why or how the spangletrees produce this fog, part gossamer and part jewel-toned dust. No birds nest in the spangletrees, and animals avoid spangletree groves. Some locals avoid the spangletrees, due to superstition, and call them Witch Trees.

The only people who enter copses of spangletrees are thieves, magicians, and perverts. Persons of low moral character congregate in the diaphanous wisps exhaled by the trees, to conduct their unsavory business.

Two such people were inside the swirling cloud on a particular evening, which was illuminated by moonlight. They prowled around the trunks. One of them carried a wand, shaped like a lightning bolt. The other had hair the color of night, contained in a braid wound with golden wire. Eventually, their paths crossed.

"Are you a sorcerer?" asked the man with a braid. He was shirtless in spite of the chill. His bronze chest was pimpled with gooseflesh. His eyes were on the wand, which emitted a wan light, casting a halo around the holder.

"Perhaps," the wand-holder replied. "Are you interested in spell craft?"

"Among other things," said the other, and suggestively stroked his crotch. And so, under the spangletrees, they shared and spilled seed by coaxing and cajoling, pulling and pushing, biting and spitting, among other things.

After the unsavory business concluded, they parted ways under cover of the sparkling mist, both of them spattered with spangles of all kinds. This was when the magician saw that he no longer had the wand.

A magician without a wand is like a eunuch.

Magic collects in the body with no means of escape. It flows through the body's systems, wreaking havoc. Oozes out of pores, corroding and transforming. The magician could feel the magic in his veins, thrumming with strange music. His right kidney became an ear, and he could hear the swoosh and swirl of bodily functions. Some other minor organ, maybe his appendix, began speaking in some hoarse language. Had it grown a mouth? He'd heard of such things. The tide of enchantment dribbled out in his body fluids. Urine changed to every color in spectrum and his sweat became iridescent bubbles. His body sprouted a single breast. Worst of all, his skin began to change. It blistered and peeled. The features beneath the skin had been recast. They were the green of chalcedony. When this happened, he knew that he didn't have long.

Shaangö was a small isle, and the town abutting the spangletree grove was tiny. Less than a week passed when the magician began hearing whispers about a madman in the town square with long black braided hair.

As he approached the square, the magician saw people moving away, gossiping and giggling about the mad fool. Over the din of the market place, he heard a hoarse voice, croaking out nihilistic nonsense.

The magician found the thief in the square's fountain, splashing around and conversing with the stone cherubs who spat out water between their lips. He held the wand in one hand. It was necrotic green. His skin on his chest had blistered, revealing a twisted star the same color as the wand, and the magician's face.

The organ in the magician's body began shrieking; he could hear it echoing in his bones.

In one quick bound, he was in the filthy water, along with the thief, who, in his magic-induced madness, was no longer quite so comely. He snatched the wand back, and yanked the thief's braid.

"Fool," the magician said, "You have doomed us both!"

Even as he spoke, more blotches of that awful green bloomed on both their bodies.

Sigilance

He could not say when he first arrived in the Yellow City. Life before entering its boundaries was blank, as smooth as unmarked vellum. He assumed that there must have been a Before, when he learned words and concepts, where he was taught these things, but where or who had helped him grow was a mystery. Maybe he had always lived in the city, had always been the same age and height. But that seemed wrong, somehow, even if it didn't particularly bother him.

The theory, that he was an outsider, a foreigner from another place would not dislodge. It was stuck like a pebble in his shoe. It was an irritant that did not rise to the level of actual pain, but was there all the same. He knew he was different than the residents in the cursed city, in almost every way. The populace was tall and willow-thin, with harsh avian features. Noses like knives, rake-like fingers. Their eyes were washed-out and somewhere between gray and pale blue. Their faces were wrinkled with worry or with age, often the two together. Their skin was dry and papery. He could see flakes of it fall off of them. The flakes of dead skin joined with the general miasma that engulfed the city.

He, by contrast, was shorter and more muscular than the city's inhabitants. His skin was browner and smoother than theirs as well, his eye color warmer, amber-brown, and free of cataracts and veins. Even his teeth were whiter. The citizens' teeth were stained yellow or brown, from rot and cigarettes and halitosis.

For the most part, the citizenry ignored him. They ignored each other, during their laconic glides down the broken cobbled streets. But every now and then, he would catch a stray scowl, or see two of the waxy beings whispering to each other while casting glances his way.

Their misery was their currency. It formed the basis of all social interaction. They spread it around. It oozed from their pores, condensed from their breath. The very air was laden with it, a different kind of humidity.

The city had a name, one with hard consonants and long vowels. No-one called it that anymore. People called it the Yellow City due to the monochromatic scheme that dominated the city. The Yellow City sat on the shores of an acidic lake with waters the color of diseased urine. The waters were cloudy and a sulfurous stench emanated from it. A dark yellow mist rose from the surface, shrouding the city. Things lived in the lake. Fish with the faces of mammals, or with fur instead of scales, or with tentacles instead of fins.

At one time, the city had been a grand place. The architectural landscape was full of obelisks, monoliths, and buildings with ornate arches. Squares and plazas had the statues and busts of beak-nosed, angular-faced men and women with the same condescending expression. A palace crouched on the hill above the city, all soaring turrets and buttresses.

All of it was crumbling. The cathedral was surrounded by stones that had fallen from its edifice. The statues had lost a feature or two—mouthless, eyeless, noseless. Even the cobbles were cracked— he had fallen on them more than once. (The other citizens ignored him, stepping over his prone body like it was one more obstacle in the landscape).

It seemed that the very city thought that he didn't belong there.

Every day was the same in the Yellow City. A bell rang, a harsh sound that reverberated throughout the city and set his teeth chattering. He would clamber down the narrow stairs of the boarding house, careful not to step on the missing steps, and join the rest of the occupants in the kitchen. There were six or eight or sometimes ten inhabitants. Their number changed daily, growing or shrinking with no rhyme or reason. They sat on hard benches at a long table, huddled over steaming bowls of grey gruel that sometimes had bits of overripe fruit or sour nuts floating in it. There was never any room at the table, regardless of the crowd size. He ate at the counter while the willowy inhabitants muttered and grunted among themselves. It seemed that they spoke a language that he was always on the cusp of understanding. But he never was able to grasp the words or the architecture of their speech. Words and phrases shifted at random.

After breakfast, he followed the crew out into the city, which was always overcast and filled with drifting mists that it was best to avoid. Once, he stepped into the path of one, and had a phlegmy cough for a couple of weeks. Sometimes, these stray phantom clouds were impossible to avoid. The citizens of the Yellow City who came into contact with them often had rashes or running noses and occasionally, weeping sores. The group shuffled and joined other citizens, all garbed in earth-toned tattered clothing on the High Street. Then, the amassed groups would break off and enter one of the hundred or so factories that lined the avenue.

As far as he could tell, each factory was more or less the same. They all made useless things. One factory would make knives and ax blades that were dull. Another made whirligigs that didn't whirl. There was a glass factory that only made cracked windows, and a furniture factory full of three-legged chairs and couches full of coils but no stuffing. He had worked in some of them. The products he made worked. Whatever foreperson was on duty would castigate him for that in that strange almost-language and chase him out with wild gesticulations. He'd been barred from at least a dozen of the factories before he realized that making broken things was the point. The citizens of the Yellow City were dedicated to nihilism. It was a guiding principle, nearly a religious practice. The whole city was a paean to rot, decay, and meaninglessness. He eventually found a factory that made children's toys. Dolls with mismatched eyes, wooden trains with square wheels, zithers and xylophones that were always out of tune. He stuffed toy griffins and cockatrices with rotting leaves and powdered glass.

He was not paid for his labor. No one was. Also, as far as he could tell, there were no children in the Yellow City. There were rumors of a couple of children existing in the palace but no one had seen the royal family in years.

Another harsh bell rang, announcing the end of the work day. He joined the crowd as they dodged the wisps of corrosive mist. The overcast sky was slightly darker than before. Dinner was yet another helping of the grayish gruel, which had chunks of overcooked meat and bitter vegetables strewn throughout.

At least he had his own room in the boarding house. The other roomers didn't want to stay with him. Probably because of his difference. His darkness, his lack of height, his incomprehensibility. He was an outsider in a city full of outsiders.

When night fell and the sky darkened, the other boarders went out. Sometimes, they didn't return. Things prowled the Yellow City at night—criminals and the amphibious denizens of the yellow lake stalked the citizens. No one mourned the disappeared. The lurking horrors did not discourage people from going out into the bleak metropolis. He never had gone outside. The misery and the ennui hadn't worn him down enough. Instead, he watched the black stars burn against the poisoned sky from his window before he drifted off to an unquiet slumber.

He saw the sigil one evening when he walked back from the toy factory. He was tired, as he had spent the day tangling up the strings of a marionette. It had been such precise, delicate work, the derangement of the puppet's movements, that his eyes were dry. When he saw the slash of color in an alleyway, he wasn't sure if it was real or not. He had grown so used to the color scheme of the city—putrid yellow, earth-brown and black—that seeing the bright pink shape was an assault on his eyes. Also strange: none of the other people in the crowd saw it. Or, at least, they ignored it. Maybe he should ignore it as well.

The next morning, the sigil was gone. Perhaps it had never existed. He didn't think about the aberration at all until he saw it again a few days later on the side of a building. He broke away from the crowd to investigate it, moving through the marching throng, all tall, thin, and garbed in dull brown robes. He pushed against them. They ignored him, even going so far as to step on his feet. If he fell, he had little doubt that they would crush him beneath their worn boots until his body was mangled. He persisted until he was at last free of the grim parade.

Up close, the pink paint seemed to glow. It was a retina-burning shade of pink, one that continued glowing after his eyes were closed. Like the sun. The shape curved like a feather or a blade. He touched it.

It burned, and chilled him, all at once. Fire-ice, Ice-fire. Then, the pink sigil vanished.

He had a dream that night. A real dream, not a nightmare. He was used to waking up to the others' night terrors, their screeches of fear. And he, too, frequently woke up, sweat-drenched and shivering, narrowly escaping the claws or beak of some lake-born horror.

This dream was different. He was in a cavernous room, possibly subterranean. Stalactites poured from a ceiling drenched in shadow. The floor was flecked with twinkling bits of mica. The floor looked like the night sky. Not the night city of the cursed city, with its stars like bruises. Rather, a fairy-tale night sky, full of stardust. He was not alone here. Scattered throughout the cavern were other people, all of them with the same dark complexion that he had. Flowing silks, form-fitting leather. Gowns and trousers encrusted with sequins, hats with feathers. He couldn't tell the gender of these brightly clothed people. He supposed it didn't matter.

They were all moving in a crowd, towards a dais at the far end of the cavern. Two of them took his hand—a bald woman in a dark green gown with a white fur trim, and a man with braided, beaded hair in a blue-and-white patterned robe. The man had flowers in his beard, and the woman had peridot earrings. He felt the warmth of their hands as they gently pulled him forward.

The stardusted floor was soft as carpet. The stalactites glowed like candles, the closer they got to the other end of the cavern.

He saw an enormous chair, framed by two pillar-like stalagmites. The chair was hewn of crystal the color of the pink sigil. The festive crowd arrayed itself around the chair in a semi-circle, and waited in silence. He could feel the excitement from the crowd well up, a beating heart, waiting to burst. What were they waiting for? He just knew that it would be miraculous, whatever it was.

A bell sounded. It was as soft as a shiver of silver. It rippled over the surface tension of the crowd.

A being appeared before the crystal chair. It came together, droplets of bright pink condensing, coming together, forming a shape that wore pink robes embroidered with the sigil. The completed figure was darker than his own skin, a rich ebony. The face of the being was startlingly beautiful, but he couldn't say why. The features were in perfect harmony with each other. Then the being—the king, the god, the angel—smiled.

The crowd in the cavern sighed as one. The sheer magnificence of that collage of dark lips and perfectly white teeth, the spark of loving-kindness from the eyes was almost too much. The regard of the pink-robed being crested over the gathering like a wave. They all drowned in it. They were all dark bubbles in a frenzy.

He woke up suddenly, as quick as a bursting bubble. He wanted to go back to that underground place, that sacred space. The euphoria was intoxicating. He closed his eyes, wanting to fall back asleep and reenter the dreamworld. See that majestic figure in pink once more. But sleep wouldn't come. His mind was racing, filled with images of dark-skinned folk in revelry, of weird rock formations and echoey paradises beneath the earth. Also, his sheets were sticky, annoyingly so.

He peeled back his sheets, and found that his small clothes were stiff with a nocturnal emission. The residue was same color as the sigil.

He didn't remember his name, or where he was from. But he remembered love and belonging. And he remembered that Hell, or the afterlife, was below the ground, and Heaven was somewhere above. Now, it appeared that was reversed. The Yellow City was a hellscape, of a kind. The existence was plodding and full of terror. It was a place where no-one understood each other. The Yellow City was diseased.

The Pink City was heavenly, even if it was in a cavern beneath the ground. He needed to descend, to sink into the earth, to find his peace.

It was a while before he saw the pink sigil again. More than a few weeks. Weeks of flavorless gruels and rotating roommates and destroying toys. Nights of restless, dreamless sleep. And evenings where he travelled up and down the High Street, searching for that glowing pink feather.

When he had visited all of the factories and their various alleys, he roamed the parks and plazas. He began searching after the darkness fell. Sometimes, he would come upon a group of criminals attacking wandering loners. He kept to the shadows, minding his own business. He was on a quest, and besides, none of the Yellow City folk seemed to care for him. Once, he tried to help a woman who had been beaten by one such group. Her eyes were swollen and her face bled. He touched her shoulder, and she snarled at him, gestured that he should leave her alone. Another time, when he wandered by the yellow lake, he witnessed a creature emerging from the putrid waters that walked like a man and had the face of a fanged fish. The thing's eyes were round orbs of black surrounded by a globe of pale bile. A scaled penis flapped between its bowed legs. If the creature saw him, it gave no indication. It stumbled into the night, on its own strange quest.

The pink sigil finally materialized on the door of an abandoned house. By this time, he had stopped sleeping and attending his "job" at the factory. What was the point? It wasn't like anyone would miss him. There was nothing particularly interesting about this house. Like all of the houses on this street and throughout the Yellow City, its materials were rotting—the windows cracked, the stones crumbling, the wood warped. He touched the sigil, and was burned by it. He entered the house, lay on the dirt floor, waiting for sleep to come. When sleep did come, his dream was even sweeter still.

If he was an ignored outcast before, he became a full-on pariah. He wandered the streets of the Yellow City, searching for the pink sigil. Eventually, he was kicked out of his boarding house. He returned from one of his nightly strolls to find that his room was now occupied by one of the gaunt and willowy folk. It didn't matter. Even the horrible meals could be skipped. Sustenance was just a habit. Actual food was not required to live in this hellish limbo.

He stopped wearing the rough brown robes. He walked the streets in just his small clothes. He lived alone, in one of the abandoned hovels near the lake. At night, he would see other monsters emerge from the soup, things with misshaped eyes or nostrils, things with fingers and whiskers, things that oozed slime, or melted in the wan moonlight. Once, he saw an octopus with wings disgorge from the lake, its tentacles wriggling in mid-air. Another time, a clear bubble rose from the center of the lake, and in the center of that bubble was a long-haired nude woman the color of rotted egg yolks. She had no face, just two stalks protruding from her head. The bubble rose up and up, into the sky until he could see it no more. The things in the lake ignored him, as did all of the denizens of this place. Perhaps they, too, were searching for their own heaven.

Sometimes, the sigil appeared on consecutive days and nights. He would have a week of dreams of erotic transcendence. Other times, months would pass, where searching for the pink feather glyph was fruitless.

Each dream of the Pink City became more intense. He explored the city, with its homes made of glittering crystal, quartz and coral and tourmaline. He shared meals with the pastel-garbed citizens. He saw the emperor-god in pink materialize in the fountains, plazas, and buildings of the city. Where the Yellow City was falling down, the Pink City was growing. Every visit would reveal a new tower or ziggurat made of fused crystal. There were creatures in the city, sleek albino cats and fluttering birds in stained-glass colors. Folk also lived in the high balconies above the city, platforms that carved out of the rock itself. Sometimes, he would tryst with the subterranean dwellers, in singles, pairs and more. Male and female, it did not matter which. And then there was the one time that the pink-robed emperor kissed him on the lips. He remembered the taste of sweet wine filling his mouth.

The Coral City was beneath the earth. There must be some way to access it.

He searched for an entrance in addition to searching for the sigil itself. He entered the palace that crouched above the city. As far as he could tell, it was abandoned. No guards barred his way. He prowled through the rooms, all of them covered in thick pollen-colored dust and cobwebs. The furniture was moldering away. He passed a room that was dominated by a large organ. The large copper pipes were full of creatures, small birds and rodents that would sometimes scamper across the rotten keyboard. Some of the bedrooms had corpses in them, skeletal bodies clothed in faded raiments that held their shape. Once, he came upon a bedroom where two crowned figures lay in an enormous veiled bed. Their ornate robes were the same color as the acidic lake.

He found the cellars, full of wine and old prisoners, but with no hidden passages.

It was hopeless. He was a wandering wraith in cursed city, forever doomed to seek the sigil.

Eventually, he found himself on a balcony that overlooked the lake. From this vantage point, he could see shadows of the things that lived there, darkness in the shape of serpents and manta rays, and other things too terrible to describe.

Then he saw the sigil. Beneath the cloudy yellow waters, burning through them. The feather glyph, beckoning him.

He didn't hesitate, not for one moment. He knew what he had to do to reach the Coral City, and its miraculous king.

He leapt from the balcony, arrowing down into the lake.

As he dissolved and corrosive acid filled his lungs, he—

The Magus Club

Lice are everywhere on the Corpse, but they are particularly populous on the Underside, between the Scrotum and the Anus. With chittering mandibles, they feast on dead flesh, tearing white flakes with their serrated jaws. The pilgrim watches an abundance of legs and translucent taupe bodies as they graze. It is beautiful, the patterns of lace and saliva they make of the scales of skin. He could watch them forever, as they slowly chew the expanse to nothingness. But he can't ignore the Call in his body. It plays over the cobweb network of his nerves, a tintinnabulation that won't end and drives him on and on.

He felt the Call as soon as he arrived on the Corpse; everyone here obeys some epic urge. His memory, his name, all vanished, to be replaced by the hideous electric itching Call that drove him across the Corpse. Over the Nipples, and the vast expanse of the Belly.

Strange cities sprouted on the rotting ground of the Corpse. Structures of bone and gristle, cemented by blood and bile, where tame lice hooked up to rickshaws patrolled narrow streets. These cities, lit by energy powered from the dying brain waves and rigor mortis, were dangerous places. They were glorified slums for criminals, ruled by cults and tyrants. Brothels full of succubae and catamites festered like infections in their alleys. The pilgrim avoided them.

The Call drove him through areas fouled by clouds of decay; he would wrap rags around his mouth as traveled through corrosive yellow mists. It drove him around craters filled with old brown-red blood. The Corpse had been tattooed; the tattoos slithered beneath the dermis, animated symbols.

He spent a month in the scabrous caves of the Nose, nesting among its grey hairs, trying to reconstruct his past, to no avail. A syllable of his name would dance on his tongue, just beyond reach. A face would hover in memory, only to fade just as quickly. Was he in some kind of hell? After a while, he grew to accept his amnesia. It had its benefits, and he was soon to discover that all who lived on the Corpse had lost their names and identities.

He traveled over the dome of the Head, where follicle-trees fell and crashed every moment. There were fewer pilgrims up here. Most of them were hermits, driven mad by their own Calls. It was in the Eye that he first heard of the Magus Club. It was rumored that sorcerers could remove the Call from people. Maybe they could restore his name.

The club lies just beyond the herd of lice. He is prepared, having encountered the wild monsters in the Pubes. During the journey on the Buttocks, he collected dried pustules, warts, and the meaty strands of hemorrhoids. He draws them out from his briefcase, waving the sores in front of him. Meat and dust. Transparent bodies pause, scent the air, and eyes that jewel the ends of antennae flicker. He tosses a wart in the air, and the herd of lice disperses, heading toward the treat. The pilgrim throws another one, and more lead lice in its direction.

Just as he is tossing the last of the encrustations, a fellow pilgrim bursts from behind a copse of pubic hair and takes advantage of the diversion. The pilgrim is annoyed, until he sees the man is followed by a louse not distracted by the bait. It trundles gracelessly, still quicker than its prey, and overtakes him. Anguished cries, the snap of bone and tendon: they are hard to ignore as he slips past the scene. The stench of voided bowels and exposed viscera rises vomit in his gorge.

The ground shakes. Another volcanic fart burbles from the Anus. The sphincter quivers, and a staircase of stench climbs the air around him. The pilgrim skirts the lips of the Anus gingerly; it is encrusted with old excrement, so he presses a rag to his nose again.

Catching his breath, the pilgrim looks around, taking in the architecture. It wavers in the perpetual twilight and never settles on a single style. The bewitched building materials are stone, wood, mortar, thatch, stucco, iron, brick at any given time. It's as if the building can't make up its mind and erases and redraws itself. The pilgrim gets dizzy focusing on the myriad nascent forms that stretch and curl before him. Gothic cathedrals collapse into suburban compounds, which erect, in turn, rusting warehouses. Hybrid forms are created: Indian temples with automatic doors; medieval monasteries sprouting the metallic fungus of satellite dishes; castles made of adobe.

Voices drift on the breeze, soft and subsonic and full of sibilance. Snatches of song, gasps of ecstasy or agony, a run of laughter all tickle his ears. The pilgrim feels the very ground beneath his feet—that shifts from dirt to flagstones to cobbles—vibrate with footsteps and their echoes. The sounds add themselves to the Call that reverberates through his brain. A clatter of pipes. A soothing female voice that bleeds into a scream. Waves that crash and hiss. Glass that vibrates then shatters. The buttery sound of a horn, the lonely cry of a loon. All fill his ears.

The pilgrim is assaulted by all sorts of smells—the antiseptic sting of industrial chemicals, rotting food, gas, overripe fruit, and flowers. Salt spray, honeysuckle, the freshness of snow, motherly vanilla, the humid smell of shit, the taste of ash in the air . . . The walls, whatever material state they are currently in, sweat the odors out.

The pilgrim stands still for a moment, adjusting himself to the swirling chaos that surrounds him, the sensory and synesthetic overload. Then he goes forward on his quest.

The door to the Magus Club is wooden, warped by time and darkened by soot and grime. A face, pocked and nude, is carved in the wood of the door. When the pilgrim approaches, the closed eyes splinter open, and a green lambency oozes forth.

-*Enter me*, the wooden face croaks in a resinous voice. And it flows down the mottled, wooden surface of the door until it is level with the pilgrim's crotch. The lips part, revealing a red, pulsating gullet. It is obvious what key he must use to enter the club. The pilgrim unbuttons his trousers and places his flaccid member down the wooden throat. The interior is smooth. The wooden lips constrict around his cock, tightening around the base. There is a rumble as the sucking mechanism commences. The pilgrim feels the velvet slipperiness and there's a flash of memory:

a face of flesh with a cleft chin slowly licking his body down to his cock, ingesting it, the strains of Nina Simone's contralto in the background, a ceiling stained with the brown islands of watermarks-
and the memory slips away.

The vibrations stop after a moment, and gears and cogs shift as the door swings open inward. The pilgrim adjusts his fly, and steps in the hallway.

The floor of the hallway is tiled in mirror, reflecting the black emptiness of the ceiling above. The walls are bone-white and luminous and cast a triptych of shadows that distort the pilgrim's every step. A few steps down the corridor, and he hears the door close behind him with a thud. The walls are as soft as flesh, and as pliant. They hold the memory of his fingerprints for a moment before smoothing out. And a flash of memory:

other flesh that held the memory of his fingerprints, a green glass ashtray overflowing with butts, bodies tangled in each other and sheets with paisley designs-

The Call is louder here than it ever was. It is now a silver, needle-thin scream that leads him down the hallways of gauze and flesh. Perhaps he will end up mad after all. The Corpse is rotting; why wouldn't it rot the minds of those who lived on its surface? He glances down in the mirror-floor, and sees his own face. The hollow eyes, the gaunt cheeks, and the sallow undertone to his dark skin: he barely recognizes himself. He is a walking corpse on the Corpse. Did death do this to him, or the Call?

The hallways of the Magus Club twist and turn like vines. The passages veer off to the left and to the right, with no logic. Rooms grow like tumors. Honeycombed through the living walls, most of them are dark and empty. But every now and then, the pilgrim will see an occupied cell, protected by a thin membrane, like a transparent eyelid.

In one cell, a photographer develops pictures endlessly. The pilgrim pauses to watch him work in his red-lit darkroom. Images of flowers and Negro genitalia emerge from chemical baths. The photographer obsessively places them on the ovoid surface of the walls, where they are absorbed. "The flowers of negritude," whispers the pilgrim.

In another cell, a black writer with the white hair of Santa Claus writes on his cell's wall. The words are backwards, dyslexic, and they vanish as each sentence is completed, slowly turning in a vista that shows a decaying industrial city lit by two moons.

The Call draws him on, past other rooms and scenes.

A group of men, gaunt and wasted, form a circle jerk and their mingled seed creates a pearl that glows. *Pearl-seed*, the pilgrim thinks. *Fathers of pearl.*

A philosopher, bald and bespectacled, reads revolutionary texts while being whipped by a boy the color of coffee with cream.

He knocks at each door, begging for entrance. The inhabitants ignore him, concentrating on their own madnesses.

The Call is unbearable now. It rings and reverberates through his body, rattling bone and brain. He turns a corner, and sees *it* in one of the honeycomb pods.

The Call.

The Call is a man made of sound. Flesh that sings, muscles that pulse, blood cells that are notes. A soundwave in human form. And another flash of memory:

bending over synthesizer modules and flickering computer screens and guitars, creating hymns to the chthonic soul within–

He was a musician. This much is clear. He took sound and shaped it. Anything and everything was his palette: the sound of insects, the voices of scholars were woven within his abstract compositions, giving life to dreams.

The shape of the man of sound is his own. It wears (or *sings*) his face. His name is hidden in the notes.

The pilgrim approaches the membrane that separates him from the thing he seeks. The membrane does not give. The pilgrim withdraws a knife from his briefcase, and pierces the stuff. It parts, and he catches a scent of the marvelous music within. The gash immediately fills, becomes whole and impenetrable and silence descends. It is a waterfall that hardens to diamond. The pilgrim beats against the no longer flexible membrane, until his palms are bloodied. His soul sits in the honeycomb cell, blissfully unaware of the tumult. The soul shimmers with decibels. The Call is louder now than it's ever been. The frequency shatters his density, separating the very cells of his body. His ears and nose begin to bleed.

The pilgrim slides down the glass doorway, leaving a smear of blood that is absorbed by the sheet of diamond, tinting it cruel pink. It is useless, his whole life or afterlife. *Curse it all. This horrible Corpse.* If he could, he would destroy it all. Weeping, on the floor of mirrors, he says a Name.

In a sound like crashing glass and falling water, the membrane falls apart. The awful Call that's followed him for ages in the dead lands ceases its ringing. The pilgrim stands and smiles, dripping blood, and steps into the cell. The cell closes again, leaving two occupants in the cool interior. The man of sound rises and approaches the man of flesh.

Face to face, they kiss. Lips locked, they devour each other, saliva and sound, until they permeate each other. Flesh and wave absorb one another.

Hybrid and hyphenate: they are a new creature, imbued with a new quest. It is the goal of all of the prisoners of the Magus Club:

What spell will resurrect the Corpse?

Spyder Threads

The SUV was shiny black, as if it had just been waxed and polished. The windows were tinted so dark that I couldn't see through them. The license plate frames had LED lighting. I don't remember the license number, but I remember that it was all letters and it was strange. All vowels or all consonants—an unpronounceable word.

It had been following me for a while as I walked from the old theater where the Sparkle Ball would be held to the fleabag hotel where I was staying a few blocks away. Maybe it was a coincidence.

It was just me and the black van in a deserted city. I didn't see a soul out in that neighborhood of boarded-up houses, cracked sidewalks, and broken windows. It could have passed by me at any time. Instead, it crept along at a snail's pace.

I stopped in the middle of an empty block, and turned to face the van.

It was silent as it drove up to me, and stopped.

The side of the van was emblazoned with a logo. A lopsided circle of vivid purple with flakes of glitter in the dark center.

Was it an eye?

Or a mouth?

An opening?

An exit?

The color of the circle was too bright. I couldn't look at it too long. But I couldn't look away, either.

The window rolled down. A fragrance oozed out of the van, perfuming the air with bergamot and licorice.

A bony-looking brother, dark and bald in sunglasses directed his gaze at me. He said, "He would like an audience with you." His voice was deep, soft and expressionless.

"Who?" I asked.

I already knew the answer.

⌐

They called him Spyder.

His couture work was legendary.

Where he was from, even where he lived, was of much conjecture. Some said the he was from the slums of Detroit. Others said that he grew up in Watts. Oakland, D.C., and Gary, Indiana were all possibilities.

Among the more fanciful: he was the unacknowledged child of one of the great designers. One indisputable fact, though, is where and when he burst on the Ballroom Scene.

It was five years ago, at the Peacock Ball, held annually in the D.C. area. That year, it was held in the basement level ballroom of the past-its-prime Imperial, which stood in the shadow of the Capitol building, in a block full of Brutalist architecture. The Imperial was in the Beaux Arts style, solemn columns, arched windows and doors, rococo cornices, statues of Diana and Dionysus in the lobby, all covered in the soot and grime of city pollution.

The Grand Salon Ballroom had been transformed into an alien landscape. Nets with balloons hung from the ceiling. Dining room tables were terraformed with colored fabrics in tones of electric blue and emerald green. House music full of shrieking divas pulsated from speakers. Stages were set at the far end of the room, with the long tongue of a catwalk extended out into the audience.

During the last runway performance, as the audience was drifting away from their seats, an announcer said over the P.A., "We have a late edition to the show. From the House of Spyder."

The houselights were on at this moment, and the dull chatter of inebriated patrons swallowed and muffled the announcement. The music began to play, a music that was different from the high energy, pulse-pounding dance music. It was becalmed, tentative piano notes held in a suspension, in a thick jelly of sound that oozed over the crowd. A chord would play, followed by rippling that sounded like white noise.

The model who took the stage looked nothing like the other models who'd pranced and vogued down the catwalk before. The Peacock Ball was fashion-based, run by a regime of fashionistas who took their cues from *Vogue*, *Marie Claire*, and the fiefdoms of

Versace and Vuitton. They had been long-limbed and lithe, like ga-
zelles, garbed in mesh and nylon and gaberdine and muslin, hooved
in stiletto heels, made up to conceal and twist their genders. This
model, though, was fat. No other euphemism was appropriate for
him—and it was undeniably a him. The beard made sure of that.

The queens in the audience were vicious when they saw him. The
words whale, hippopotamus, and hog floated about the gathering,
as if it were a schoolyard.

But when the model stepped into the spotlight, a hush came over
the crowd, a silencing wave, so all that was heard was the droning
hum of the music. The lower part of the gown was made of wood, or
so it appeared. The silver ash of birch bark, punctuated with sickle
marks of the wood beneath. Rising out of the trunk of the gown
were branches, which seemed to be living, as these wiry digits were
bejeweled with leaves of acid green fabric. The model's bearded face
was surrounded by a nimbus of leaves and white branches.

The birch tree-model glided down the runway, graceful as a
dancer. The weight of his body, and of the outfit, were nothing to
him. In fact, as the gargantuan man went down the aisle, it was impossible to imagine anyone else wearing the couture outfit. This was
the daily wear of a god or some mythological being.

The birch-tree god came to the end of the runway. Some say that
the model bowed and at that moment, the leaves changed from
green to gold through some optical illusion. Others say that a sudden wind (possibly from a backstage fan) blew and scattered the
leaves over the audience.

But I was there that night.

I saw the large queen stand on the edge of the catwalk and freeze.
The lights went out for a heartbeat or two. And when the houselights
went up, a real birch tree somehow grew out of the ballroom floor.

The fumes in the van were so strong that my eyes watered. I asked
the driver to open a window. He ignored me. He might have been a
robot, or made of stone. He wore a dark suit that sparkled as if there
were chips of mica embedded in the fabric.

We drove through the city, past industrial warehouses, dockyards,
and seemingly empty office towers. There was a web of phone wires

slicing the grey sky into ribbons. Factory smoke stacks belched out blue clouds of pollution. Maybe keeping the windows shut was the better option.

I got a headache just the same, drowning in a sea of citrus and anise aroma. The A/C was on full blast and so cold that I saw little puffs of breath.

What had made me get into the van, anyway? I must have had a death wish. After all, everyone who wore one of Spyder's threads seemed to vanish. People thought it was because of some ironclad NDAs.

I didn't think that was the reason.

Maybe it was the cold or the intensity of the reeking van, but I zoned out as we passed empty streets.

I had followed Spyder from ball to ball, coast to coast. From Chi-town to Motor City, D.C. to Philly, Newark to Watts. In empty warehouses and on theatre stages. I might have seen all of his outfits. Like the skirt he made of writhing snakes. The veil made of discarded cauls. The bustier made of finger bones. Spyder never disappointed. Each outfit was more outrageous than the last one. But I didn't follow him just because I loved his work.

I wasn't just obsessed like some stupid Yeezy or Jay-Z groupie. It was deeper than that. Can you feel me? You see, it was my dream, my aspiration, to wear a Spyder outfit. To be one of his models!

At San Francisco's Chimera Ball, the model walked on forearm crutches, (apparently, he had multiple sclerosis). The corset was constructed of honeycombs, still dripping with royal jelly. The close-fitting skirt seemed to have writhing masses of honeybees. Some of them crawled on the model's crutches, leaving gold-dust pollen on them. Several attendees swore that they had been stung.

In autumn of that year, at Chicago's Chthonian Ball, the dress was seashells: conches, cowries, abalones, junonias and numerous others. The model had *ichthyosis vulgaris*, a condition that turned his skin into scales. Barnacles rested in his cornrowed hair. He embodied Oceanus himself. Many of the attendees of the Chthonian Ball, held in a shabby K-town hotel, swore they smelled the salty air of the sea and that a dampness pervaded the ballroom. The organizers were banned from using the hotel afterwards, due to the appearance of mildew on the flocked wallpaper and the outdated industrial green carpet.

Spyder's models were all outside of the beauty standard. He celebrated and elevated otherness.

The van slowed down at a gate. Behind the gate were a cluster of corrugated tin storage units. The driver rolled down the window, releasing some of the perfumed air and punched in a code in a keypad. The gate opened with a pneumatic groan, and we went forward.

"How did Spyder know that I'd be at the Sparkle Ball?" I asked.

The sparkly-bony man didn't answer. He just drove and parked the SUV in front of a unit, one that was indistinguishable from any of the others.

I was frightened. I could hear the blood pounding in my ear. I was also excited. Exhilarated, even.

The driver led me down the narrow path between two putty-colored units and unlocked a nearly invisible door.

My heart leapt up into my throat when the door opened.

I began staying after the shows, when the sets were dismantled, hoping to catch a glimpse of the illusive figure. Was he the dude decked out in Dior? The thin man in the navy Burberry coat? Was he the thick queen in a mesh shirt, lipstick, guy liner, and a diamond-encrusted grill? No, no, and no.

Then, I changed my tact. I tried cornering the models who were Spyder's creations after the shows. I could never catch up with them. Maybe they left immediately after their performances. I trawled the dressing rooms and backstage areas, finding them empty.

The only one I managed to speak with was after the Flower Ball, held in San Francisco. The Ball was held in an abandoned warehouse in SoMa. The dude was maybe 6'5" or even 7 feet tall. A real Watusi. Spyder had outfitted him in pantsuit made of lady slipper orchids that seemed to grow out of his skin, as if he were some kind of living mangrove tree. I saw him hanging around backstage. I offered to buy him a drink.

We found a dive bar nearby, catering to the S&M crowd. A giant and a dwarf weren't the strangest pair in that place, if you know what I mean. We got no second looks.

I asked him, "When did you meet Spyder?" when we were sitting at the bar.

He said, "Who?"

"Quit playing."

He gave a blank stare, one that was genuinely confused. "Who da fuck is Spyder?"

I tried not to roll my eyes. "You know. The dude whose outfit you wore. The one who dressed you."

"Oh," he said. Something by Drake came on through the speakers. The model, whose name was Levi, started swaying on his stool and mouthing the words. "I don't remember anyone named Spyder," he finally said.

"Really?" I said. "I mean, who pasted those flowers on your body? That must have taken hours."

Levi glanced at me, then away, to the light show of green and purple beams that wavered over the dance floor. I saw men in black dog masks. Men in leather caps and harnesses. Men dressed like the police, or S.S. Officers. It was creepy.

But not as creepy as the look that Levi gave me.

I don't quite know how to explain it. He leaned towards me, getting ready to speak to me. But then, he froze. It was like he had a mini-stroke. His face went slack, and his eyes, I swear to God, changed color. Just for a moment. Maybe even less. They went from dark brown around black irises to violet. Like Elizabeth Taylor's eyes supposedly were. Then Levi leaned back, as if nothing had happened.

I asked him about Spyder again.

He opened his mouth, about to speak. Something fell out of his mouth.

A petal, yellow with scarlet stripes, covered in a gooey, sticky substance.

I said his name.

Another cobwebbed petal fell out, followed by another. And another.

"Are you okay?"

Levi left me to go the bathroom, roughly pushing aside the men in the bar.

I waited the length of a song before I went into the bathroom.

Levi was gone. The trough urinal, though, was full of urine, ice, and browning flower petals.

Behind the door was a set of metal stairs that went down. I couldn't see the bottom, and there were no lights. The bony-sparkly man said, "Come on. He's waiting." He held a flashlight in his hand, which he switched on. It did not illuminate anything. Then he went down the stairs, his footsteps echoing.

This was what I wanted. What I needed. I wanted to be beautiful, if only for one moment. To be bathed in the spotlight, adored by the crowd. I was unloved. Kicked out of my home at sixteen, not pretty enough or tall enough or pale enough to fit into gay culture. Queens can be vicious. I was called a midget, or Gary Coleman. But if I were outfitted in one of Spyder's threads, I could transcend my defects. Be elevated and celebrated. That was worth whatever terrible thing that happened to other models, wasn't it?

We went down and down, the flashlight's beam bouncing against cinderblock. The flights of stairs seemed to be endless, and it was dizzying. How far underground were we? It defied logic.

My eyes adjusted to the darkness to the point that the bony-sparkly man's flashlight was unneeded. He did not remove his sunglasses, for some reason.

The smell of the SUV—bergamot and licorice—drifted up. And, at last, I could see the end of this descent.

The sub-sub-sub-basement was a chamber to the right of the column of stairs. I looked up, got Escher vibes at the interlaced metal mesh that I'd just come down. Was this some forgotten bunker or nuclear fallout shelter? The stairs were a tower that tunneled upwards, leaving the surface world forever out of reach. I was tired, just thinking about going back up.

The driver gestured me to enter the chamber. I hesitated. The smell was so strong that I could almost see the haze of fumes. It was like a perfume factory on steroids.

I stepped into the chamber. Alone.

The walls of the room were concrete hung with scattered capsule-shaped light sconces. The floor I stood upon was metal grating, like you would find in an abattoir. In the center of the room was a mound of dirt that was roughly in the shape of an anthill. But it wasn't made of mounded dirt. It was made of some substance that resembled puckered flesh. A pale violet mist trickled from the hill.

I crept toward this, against my better judgment, to get a better look—

"Don't get too close," someone said. The voice came from *within* the pit.

I stepped back. Far back, almost to the chamber door.

A hand emerged from the pit. Followed by another hand. And another. And another.

Until a tall, thin man with too many appendages was up and out of the mound.

How tall was he?

How thin?

How many arms did he have? And how long were they?

I did not see a nose or mouth. Just tiny beadlike eyes that were black.

What I saw was incoherent and hard to look at. He was a blur of motion, with stick-like arms and legs, and a long thin face. He reminded me of a daddy longlegs.

"Spyder," I said. And in saying his name, his shape's frenzy stilled. He was still too tall and too thin, but he had the correct number of hands and eyes.

"I love your work," I stammer like a starstruck teenager.

"Oh, honey chile, I know. I had my eye on you for a while." His voice has a smooth, narcotic quality, aural cough syrup.

"How do you make such wondrous outfits?" I say. It sounds stupid and pedestrian. "You're better than all of the designers— Balenciaga, Lagerfeld, Gauthier . . . Did you go to Parsons, or . . ."

He laughs. His black eyes sparkle with violet glitter.

"Oh, doll," he says to me. "You are about to see how the magic is done."

In this hollow, echoing room, I find no evidence of fashion design. No mannequins, no rolls of fabric, no sewing machines.

As I undress, he speaks:

"When I was a child, I saw a the most marvelous movie I'd ever seen. It was called *Mahogany*. Maybe you've heard of it. It's the story of a young department store clerk who becomes a fashion model, and eventually, a designer. The plot is basically a morality play in which the designer gets enmeshed in the decadent world of couture fashion. Not that interesting. But the displays of fabric and the shapes of clothing that could be created from them imprinted my young soul. It was a spiritual awakening. My soul had been plain white linen. The movie soaked that linen, dyed it a rich vibrant hue, and changed the composition of its fabric to a rich satiny finish.

"In the movie Diana Ross was transformed into Mahogany, a high priestess of fashion . . .

"The universe, of course, is a black and cold place. And if it cares not for humanity, what are the dreams of little sissy black boys to it? I learned this the hard way, when Mommy and Daddy kicked little old me out of their Good Christian nest."

Spyder takes my hand, and walks me up to the geyser.

"Ah, my diminutive muse, the universe *did* listen to this faggot's *crie du coeur*. It gave me access to the most marvelous thing in existence. Meet Mahogany." He gestures grandly to the puckered abyss.

He embraces me in his many, many arms, and jumps—

I am bathed in the essence of bergamot and licorice. It flows around me, licking my unloved body. Tasting and penetrating every crack and orifice.

In the grape darkness, I feel them. The industry of Spyder's arms and fingers coiling around my naked form. They cocoon me in satiny, shimmering fabric around my form in a haphazard, zig-zagging way as I hang there. Every contour of my body, sans face, arms, and feet, is covered in cobwebs made of light.

The dress seems to be a living thing. It breathes, like a rising chest. It is made of feathers, thousands of them stitched together like wings. The iridescent gray of pigeons, the snow-white of doves, the technicolor scream of parakeet wings. Where the bones of the wings meet, there are eyeballs. Human eyes of blue, sea-green, earth-brown, hazel, and grey. Eyes that are speckled like eggs, and eyes that have the frost of glaucous glaze. There are also the eyes of cats, slits in pools of primrose and topaz. The eyes of birds—the hot yellow of eagles, the beadlike eyes of sparrows. The silhouette of the gown is striking; it looks like it's about to take flight. And in the searing spotlight, the eyes appear to blink.

The music that accompanies my catwalk is made of breath and wing flutters and coos.

All of the eyes are on me, and for one shining moment, I am the angel of the Sparkle Ball. I am beautiful, am Beauty itself.

When the runway walk ends, I stand in front of the spangled lavender curtain. I make a final gesture. The spotlight extinguishes.

Then, I flex my many wings, and take flight.

Desiccant

The Bellona Heights Apartments were rundown. The pavement of the open semi-courtyard had cracks, concrete wounds that oozed out moss and straggling weeds. An old fountain, spattered with bird droppings, was filled with stagnant rainwater and trash. The first-level beige brick had graffiti, scrawls of obscene words and nonsense shapes scrawled across it. The balconies that faced the courtyard were over-stuffed with plants, bicycles, and rusting lawn furniture. The cornices were crumbling. Hip hop and Reggaeton blasted from open windows.

Tituba shuddered in revulsion. But she had no choice, did she?

You get what you pay for, she thought, and a one bedroom in Bellona Heights was what she could afford. At least she'd found a place to live on such short notice. Her sister's new boyfriend Vaughn had threatened to change the locks one too many times. Tituba loved her sister Leah, but her choice in men was terrible. At least Juan, the last one, didn't misgender her. Yes, this place was below her standards, but, she reasoned, the lease was only for one year. And surely, she could find a more suitable place by then?

Inside the building, Tituba saw worn linoleum and the chipped paint on the walls. She picked up her keys at the office from a sullen clerk who couldn't pull her eyes away from a game on her phone, and rode the old gear-winding elevator up to the fourteenth floor. Phantom odors drifted down the hallway, weed, old fried fish, and, of course, boiled cabbage. Boiled cabbage was the smell of despair and deferred dreams.

1412 was semi-furnished, with a futon/couch frame and dresser-drawers. It was on the other side of the building, so there was no balcony. The window faced the alley, which was full of dumpsters.

At least it was clean, for the most part. The only visible flaw was the discoloration right outside the air-conditioning vent. Carmine smears dribbled from the grate. Tituba touched it before she thought better of it. She felt a powdery dust on her fingertips, surprised to find that it was not dried paint or even worse, blood.

Fabiana was late, as she always was. Tituba had been sitting at the cafe for a good fifteen minutes. She entered the space with a dramatic flair, her face wrapped in a bright orange scarf, and wearing bejeweled sunglasses. Her hands were encased in some silvery gloves. Heads turned, whispers came up from the other tables. She always wanted to be noticed. While Tituba had her moments, for the most part she wanted to be left alone.

Fabiana air-kissed her and then ordered an Americano and a low-fat blueberry muffin. She ignored both of the items.

"How's the new place? And when's the housewarming?" Fabiana asked her as she removed her sunglasses, revealing violet-colored contact lenses.

"The place is ratchet, so there will not be a housewarming party. Leah and that scrub Vaughn practically tossed me out into the street."

"I thought Leah had your back," Fabiana said.

"She usually does," Tituba said, "when she's not dick-a-matized. Vaughn pitched a fit when one of his boys asked him for my number. He threw around the words, 'she-male,' and tranny and accused me of flirting. Leah didn't stop him. She became a whole other person. Meek and useless."

"Girl, if he had called *me* those names, I'd have sliced him up. I still carry my knife, in case anyone is fixing to get smart with me!"

"Trust me, it got ugly. He was all, 'What type of crazy name is Tituba?' Frankly, I was angrier at my sister than I was at him. I felt betrayed."

"I'm so sorry for you," Fabiana said. "Do you want me to do something to teach this dude a lesson? I know some people."

"No," she replied. "I guess this is part of my journey. I thought I'd lucked out and wouldn't have to go through people around me rejecting who I was."

"I don't blame you," Fabiana replied. She finally ate a bite of her muffin. A tiny bird bite. "You sleeping all right?" she asked.

"No . . . Why do you ask?"

"Them bags under your eyes, child. You know what will fix them? Hemorrhoid cream. It tightens the skin."

"I am not about to put ass cream under my eyes!" Tituba said. Both of them laughed loudly, causing the other café patrons to glance in their direction.

Fabiana said playfully, "Keep it classy, bitch!"

Tituba swatted at her hand. "Oh, hush. Seriously, though. Falling asleep isn't the problem. Hell, *staying* asleep isn't, either. I sleep, but I wake up tired, as if I had a tough work out at the gym, or gone a few rounds with a boxer. And when I wake up, there's always some weird reddish dust on me. And it's not just me. My neighbors all look—drained. One day, I saw a kid at the bus stop and his collar had stains of that red dust."

"Huh," said Fabiana. "Have you heard about Sick Building Syndrome? It's a place where all of the occupants get headaches and permanent sniffles. And fatigue. I think the Post did a series about it—one of the buildings owned by the EPA had it, and they had to close it."

"The *effing* Environmental Protection Agency had a 'sick building?'"

"You have to get out of there," Fabiana said, "Or, you need to get all *Norma Rae* on the building supervisor!"

Dust! Miles and miles, dune after dune of rust-red, as far as her eye could see. A red that was the color of old blood, slowly changing from crimson to brown.

She stood knee-deep in the middle of a valley, surrounded by mounds of the stuff. The sky above was hidden, obscured by a veil of red powder. She was sinking under, unable to get purchase on the feathery ground. The clothes she wore were reduced to blood-stained rags. It looked like she was shedding a membranous skin, like a snake. Her skin had abrasions, a network of thin cuts that were crusted over and flaking.

She must move on, before being swallowed whole by the wavering ground. If she didn't move, she would drown and die, forever preserved beneath, a beautiful mummy no-one would ever see. She must move, or else she would die.

She lifted one foot clear of the squelching redness. And the wind began to blow. Dust rose up into the air, into a corrosive mist that erased her body. Soon, she could not see anything. All was lost in the simoom.

Tituba woke up coughing. Her body shuddered with the fit. She could feel something rattling in her chest, as if her body were a percussion instrument filled with dry rice or sand. After the fit was over, she got up and switched the light on. Her tongue was heavy in her mouth, so she stumbled to the sink and drank two full glasses of water before she felt relatively normal.

She put the glass in the sink, checked the time. It was 3:30 A.M., early enough for a second shift of sleep. But she was too wired to get back into her bed. And, it seemed that she wasn't the only person up at this hour. The floor above her creaked with footsteps. Bellona's paper-thin walls revealed activity on either side of her apartment, coughing on the left, the plaintive voice of a distressed child on the right.

Tituba knew that falling back to sleep would be difficult, so she pulled her phone from her charging port. Her headphones were on the ottoman next to her futon. That's when she first noticed the red dust. It was all over her mattress and futon, a fine sifting of rust-colored powder. She touched it. It didn't feel of anything. It was not coarse or smooth. It was feathery and insubstantial, even though she expected it to have a gritty feel like sand or salt. Then, it moved. An infinitesimal slither through her fingers, a blur of micro-movement. Reflexively, Tituba shook the stuff off her fingers and headphones.

It wouldn't come off. There was a slight disturbance, but then the powder-dust settled back. It clung to the curve of the headphones, the whorl of her fingertips. Tituba rubbed at the dust, hoping to dislodge it with friction. That did not work. Her fingertips were stained.

She muttered a curse word or two under her breath. She ran water over the stubborn stain at the kitchen sink.

A piece of dried skin, embossed with a fingerprint, fell off her hand, leaving behind tender new skin. She watched as the opaque red crinkled skin settled in the sink.

The powder-dust plumped up with the water. Fat with sudden moisture, the flakes began to rise upward, as if buoyed by an unfelt breeze. Red drops of old blood hung in the air, hovered. Then, they burst open.

Tituba screamed.

The office door was locked, as it had been for the past two weeks. Tituba had stopped by the superintendent's office before and after work, on the weekend, but the door had always been locked. The emails she sent were unanswered, and the phone calls went straight to voice mail.

She didn't know if she'd even seen him during the time she'd been in Bellona Heights. Her neighbors confirmed that he was elusive and unreachable at the best of times. Everyone she'd spoken to had given her a "why bother" attitude. When she told the residents in the mailroom or lobby about the mysterious, weird dust she'd seen, they just shrugged, as if defeated.

One time in the laundry room, she asked Phylis, an older woman who lived on the same floor, if she knew anything . . .

Phylis had been folding a child's clothes when Tituba had entered the shabby basement with a week's worth of dirty clothing. Phylis had grudgingly given her a greeting when Tituba broached the subject.

"Yeah, I've seen it," Phylis had said, dripping with attitude. "Folks made a stink about it, back in the day. Nothing happened."

"But it must be unhealthy. So many people here have respiratory problems."

"And?" Phylis said, as she went to unload a dryer that had just buzzed. "Ain't nobody who owns this glorified flophouse care about our health. This ain't Northwest."

Tituba purposefully ignored the bitterness dripping from Phylis's voice. "Maybe not. But the dust isn't natural. I hear it rattling in the vent, like tiny ants. Like it's alive . . ."

Phylis stopped folding the laundry and threw it into the basket. "You're a fine one to talk about 'unnatural' things," she announced as she headed to the door.

Tituba said, "Excuse me?"

But Phylis was already out of the room.

Now, she stood in front of the office door for the umpteenth time. She jiggled the lock, even though she knew there was no point. Maybe Phylis was right, and she should leave well enough alone. But she couldn't. Tituba's entire existence had been full of struggle, starting from birth, and it didn't look like it was going to get easy any time soon. The dancing dust was just one more obstacle to overcome.

Tituba went to the mailroom instead. She found the tiny room was full of packages and guessed that some of them were nebulizers and humidifiers. All week long, residents had unboxed the machines in the room, leaving a pile of broken-down cardboard boxes. She had toyed with getting one herself, to combat the dryness in the building.

Fabiana was right. Bellona Heights was a sick building. Ever since she'd moved in, she had been plagued with low-key headaches that threatened to grow in to full-on migraines. Her stomach was unsettled, and food tasted weird. Walking down a city block easily winded her. And she began to notice discolorations on her skin: darkness beneath her eyes, and white spots on her arms. Most of all, she was always thirsty. She would drink bottle after glass of water or juice but she could never be satisfied. She didn't pee often, for the amount she drank. Where did it all go?

She passed by the superintendent's door, in futile hope.

"Warren not in again?" said someone behind her. It was Ty, who also lived on her floor. He was around her age and height, with a muscular, lithe physique. His skin was dark and velvet-smooth, his bald head glowing with head wax. At least, that *had* been his appearance. Now, crow's feet and forehead wrinkles marred the smooth expanse, and the lustrous blue-blackness of his skin was dried out to a leathery brown.

"Apparently not." Tituba looked away from Ty, hoping that he didn't notice her shocked reaction.

He jiggled the doorknob, as if to verify. Then, he glanced at Tituba, and gave her a conspiratorial wink.

"Desperate times," he said, and he pushed against the door with his shoulder. The door quivered with the pressure and after a few more aggressive pushes, it popped open.

Ty and Tituba were immediately hit with a wave of stale air that had a slight cindery taste. They simultaneously began coughing in response. There was also another smell beneath that one—a smell of turned meat and the coppery tang of old blood. A haze of carmine simmered in the room, thick enough that they both had to wave it away. The shades were drawn, so it was dim in the room.

"Oh, my god," Tituba said, after her eyes adjusted to the gloom.

There was a body slumped over a desk. She knew that it was a corpse. The angle of the head looked too uncomfortable to maintain, and the visible eye was open. She switched on the overhead light and immediately wished that she hadn't. The older gentleman was in a grey mechanic's suit, and his mouth was opened in a grimace. Dust pooled around the open mouth, onto the desk. It was embedded on his skin, in his hair, and she could see flecks of it in the whites of his eye.

Ty walked around the desk, reached out to touch the body.

"Leave it alone," Tituba said.

Ty lowered his hands, and reached for his cellphone instead, presumably to call for an ambulance.

Tituba saw the wrinkled flesh, fold upon fold of thin skin, some of it so dry that the pigment had leeched out. It didn't look like skin. It was papery, cracked like old parchment. And in the folds of skin, remnants of the red dust gathered. His mouth was open and a crumbled pink tongue lolled out past black and cracked lips.

"He looks like a mummy," Ty said after he finished speaking to the emergency operator. "I wonder how long he's been here."

Tituba heard him, but she was distracted by the thin trail of red dripping down from the HVAC vent.

Whatever lived there had drained the superintendent, had turned him into a husk. His skin had the same color and texture as a tamarind. She could only imagine the poor man's innards, the pulp toughened into sponge and coral.

"He's been sucked dry," Tituba said. "We're gonna end up like him."

With tweezers, Tituba scraped the red residue into an old nail polish bottle she had cleaned out. Something was in the vents, something that left behind this weird substance.

She brought the bottle with her to dinner at a restaurant.

The first thing Fabiana said when she saw Tituba was, "Girl, you look ashy and worn out!"

"I know," she replied, waving the comment away. "Listen to me. You were right. Bellona Heights *is* a sick building. Some kind of virus or something *lives* in the vents and gives everyone who lives there breathing problems!

"Last week, one of the other residents and I found the superintendent dead in his office. His body was dry. Bone dry. Desert dry. All of the moisture had been sucked right out of him."

Tituba pulled up a picture on her phone, and handed it to Fabiana.

Fabiana shrieked. "Put that thing away!"

Tituba complied.

Fabiana said, "I don't think I've ever seen anything so terrible. Poor dude. He looks like one of those apple head dolls."

"I asked the EMTs if they were gonna do an autopsy to determine the cause of death. They ignored me."

Fabiana sucked her teeth in sympathetic dismay. "They always do. And we end up dead because they won't listen!"

Tituba dug around in her handbag until she found and pulled out the nail polish bottle.

"Look at it, Fab. Look closely."

"Look at an empty bottle of Carolina Beet lacquer?" Fabiana cautiously picked the bottle up, and peered into it.

"Stop kidding around, girl. Tell me what you see."

Fabiana stared at it for a long moment, still looked as the server refilled their wine glasses with Rosé.

Finally, she said, "That dust moves."

"I'm glad you saw that too! I thought I was going crazy!"

Fabiana still held the bottle close to her eye. "I don't think it's dust, Tituba. I saw one fragment of whatever-it-is, apart from the others, move on its own. I see wings. Tiny, infinitesimal scarlet wings. The wings of a moth, not a butterfly. The straggler eventually joined the rest of the swarm, I suppose. And it looked like a swirling dust."

"You think it's insects?"

Fabiana shrugged in response. "I don't know. All I do know is, you have to get the hell out of there!"

¤

Tituba was unlocking the door to her apartment when she heard the scream. It came from down the hall. She found herself running there and knocking on the door until Phylis, the grandmother who lived there with her daughter Krystle and grandson Kendrick, opened it.

"What's wrong, Miss Phylis?" she asked.

Miss Phylis was wild-eyed and apoplectic, apparently unable to speak. She gestured weakly to an opened doorway off the L-shape of the apartment. More screams came from there, mostly Krystle saying, "Lord, lord, lord!" Tituba left Miss Phylis behind to look in the doorway.

She tried to make sense of the bizarre scene. This was obviously a child's room, full of Thomas the Tank Engine paraphernalia, the google-eyed train's face on toys and curtains and posters, with its frozen smile stretched across the face. The walls were splattered with moving constellations that came from a projector lamp. Tituba saw little Kendrick being cradled by his mother, in what looked like a grotesque parody of the Pietá, his limp body draped over her lap. His eyes were closed and fluttering, as if he were fighting to keep them open, some nightmare thing wouldn't let him wake up. Things moved on his unconscious body. Scarlet specks, a tide of them spilling over his pajamas, arms, and face. The tiny little blister-colored things vibrated as they moved. And they moved with purpose, heading for his nostrils and slightly opened mouth. She imagined the minuscule coating of his nasal passages, flurrying in the chambers of his sinuses, ricocheting and embedding themselves in spongy alveoli as they drank up the mists of the boy's body, drying out mucus membranes, turning plasma into dust. She heard Kendrick begin to wheeze, heard the raspy rattling in his chest.

Those creatures have done the same thing to me, every night, she thought. She recalled her dreams about Martian-red deserts and dust storms.

She switched on the overhead light. The stars became invisible. The moth-things slowed down, and lazily detached themselves from the child's body. They drifted upward, red motes of dust, heading toward the ceiling, heading toward the grates of the vent. More of them dribbled from Kendrick's nose and mouth. It looked like a twinkling river of blood. Tituba dug around her purse until she found a bottle of spray lotion. She spritzed the red-speckled air with the thick mist, saturating it. A clump of the things fell from the air, a worm-like wriggling ball of red paste with the consistency of snot. The coagulated mess fell on the floor with a wet splat. Tituba, Krystle and Miss Phylis watched with disgust at the wet wings flexing in globules of oily lotion.

Tituba said, "Quick! We have to get the rest of the stuff out of Kendrick! Wake him up and make him drink water. Maybe that will flush them out."

Krystle carried Kendrick into the kitchen, where he blinkingly woke up in the harsher light. They got the confused child to slurp down a couple of glasses of water. Then he began coughing, body-wracking spasmodic coughs. His mother patted his back, calling Kendrick her little angel, her sweetheart, her precious boy.

Then, he vomited.

Out of his mouth came a stream of red paste. They saw the fragments of wings and waterlogged pieces of something drip onto the floor. The swarm of dust-insects was decimated. But more lived in this forgotten, neglected building full of brown and black bodies. Were these tiny, moth-like vampires conscious of what they did as they fed upon sleeping bodies, draining the moisture of breath, crawling down throats? Perhaps they weren't malevolent, these winged specks of decay.

Bellona Heights. More like Hellona Depths.

Back in her apartment, Tituba blocked the vent with a piece of plywood. It was a temporary measure. She thought of black mold, or Legionnaire's bacteria brought to life with some dark magic. She thought about contacting the press or an exterminator. But people ignored the superintendent's death, and the complaints brought by the other residents. It was unlikely that anyone would listen to a Black trans woman.

She would have to fix this on her own. Survival was in her DNA. Survival, and its importance, was why she chose her name. Titus, her birth name, had been meek and a victim of the church, his family, and society. Titus would have succumbed to the dust-moths and been one more epidemiological statistic to be ignored.

Tituba, however, would fight. She would survive, like the historical woman she'd named herself after.

As she lay down at 4:00 A.M., exhausted from saving Kendrick's life, she heard the scarlet moths skittering around in the blocked vents, banging against the plywood barrier.

"I dare you," she said.

And she began coughing. Violence was in her lungs, her chest, her throat, her head. She coughed so hard that black spots appeared before her. *Some of those things must've found their way into me.* The malevolent red moths were attacking her, with clear intention. It could not have been a coincidence. They had heard her issued challenge, and now they responded.

If—when—Tituba survived this assault, she would destroy the miniature dust-demons. She would kill them *tonight*.

Sacred She-Devil

Ruby Spurlock was the third sister murdered in as many months. According to the article, Ruby had been found in a remote area of Rock Creek Park with her neck slit, and there was evidence of sexual violence. The article, like so many papers, opted to use Ruby's deadname, a final violation of her memory. One officer made a point of mentioning how "people like Mr. Spurlock were known to engage in illicit sex work," and that such work had inherent risks.

Opal sighs, disgusted and weary at the same time. But she doesn't indulge in the emotion for too long. There is much important work to do.

She lights a homemade candle, shaped like a pyramid and infused with the essence of lavender and rosehips. The flame dances, an orange teardrop in the darkness. Behind the candle is the altar of Pomba Gira, the sacred prostitute. On a wooden shelf, there is a chalice filled with cachaça upon which float rose petals. Two aspects of the Pomba Gira sit on either side of the silver cup. A doll with smooth brown skin and a frizzy cloud of hair stands on the right side, clad in an opened crimson cloak that reveals her unashamed nudity. A necklace of skulls encircles her neck. On the left side is a doll with skin the same color as the other one's cloak. She is also nude, with two horns jutting from her forehead. The candle flame's flicker animates both figures.

Opal says, "Ruby Spurlock, please come to me. This is a safe place. A sanctuary for gender warriors!"

Silence, like a dip in pressure, mantles the room. The flame flutters and distorts the shape of the dolls, stretching and squashing the attendant shadows. Opal feels tingles in her spine, a rill of needles.

Someone is listening.

Opal begins to sing Ruby's name over and over, turning the syllables into a joyous tune, a celebration of Ruby's life.

The flames dance to the rhythm of the invocation.

The shadows of the two aspects of Pomba Gira merge into one shadow, a shape both voluptuous and demonic—a horned silhouette of a goddess. The skin on both the dolls becomes dewed with moisture, and no longer porcelain or plastic but skin-like. Skin in tones of obsidian and ruby. The room fills with the scent of incense, redolent of nutmeg and allspice. Already warm, the humidity in Opal's room grows until her forehead is beaded with sweat. Darkness thickens in one corner of the room into the shape of a woman.

"Oh, Ruby," says Opal, "my sister, don't be shy. Show me how fabulous you are!"

Color blooms on the darkness, slowly resolving itself into tones. The finished woman doesn't completely materialize. She's transparent and beautiful, a tracery on the gloom.

Ruby Spurlock has red-brown skin and long box braids that fall to her waist. She's in white culottes and a mint-green peasant blouse.

Ruby takes a tentative step forward. "What is this place?"

"This is my apartment. And, as I said, a sanctuary."

"How did I get here? And, why do I feel so weird? It feels like I'm on Special K. You didn't drug me, did you?"

Opal stands up, moves towards the apparition. "How much do you remember?"

"What do you mean?" Ruby says.

Sometimes this happened. A soul would block out the trauma of their passing. For most, it was a blessing. Sequestered in the afterlife, they moved through memories, traveling through time and space, with mood the only compass. How and why they crossed over was not relevant, so it was often forgotten. Opal had no desire to reintroduce the violence of Ruby's death, but it had to be done. Other lives were at stake.

"Forgive me, Ruby. For waking you up. But I'm gonna need you to remember your last moments."

"My last moments?" Ruby says, her tone halfway between amused and terrified. "I can't feel my legs or arms. You must have drugged me!"

"No, darling. I'm afraid to tell you that you have passed away . . ."

The shade of Ruby flutters like a moth against a lit candle. Her form wobbles and blurs.

"Stay with me, Ruby. I need to hear your story."

Memory seems to come back to her. Her face crumbles, overwritten with terror. Widened eyes see something that Opal cannot. Ruby's face blooms with bruises, and her skin splits, leaking blood. Her eyes blink in rapid succession as her murder plays out once more on her phantom flesh. Opal wants to look away, but she cannot. Ruby is a Sister, and it's Opal's duty to guide her through this experience, to bear witness. So she watches the violation, a weird pantomime, sees each shiver of terror and gasp of despair as death rains down on Ruby's body. Her skin records each imprecation, becoming a testament to abuse. The monster who did these depraved acts is invisible, seen only by Ruby. It seems to go on forever, until the light in Ruby's eyes fades out.

Then Ruby is no longer in that terrible moment. She has not survived, now exists in another form.

"The motherfucker raped and killed me," she says, her voice wavering much like her spectral form.

"I'm so sorry you had to relive that, sister," Opal says. "I wish I could hold you, and comfort you—"

"Oh, yeah?" Ruby says. She's now more shadow than image, hidden in the corner of the room. "If I could, I would kick your ass. I was at peace when you pulled me here to your little shitty hovel. I was in Paris, walking down a runway beneath the Eiffel Tower, wearing a couture outfit. People were clapping for me, and handing me bouquets. I was a fucking supermodel! Then you had to drag me back here to remind me that I was killed by some maniac."

"I'm sorry, sister, but—"

"I am *not* your sister. You are way too common to hang out with the likes of me. Send me back!"

Opal stands, suddenly feeling shabby in her floral house dress. Her hair is unbrushed and hidden beneath a red headwrap. She has a faint mustache that won't go away, even with all of the hormones she's taken. She is far from being fashionable.

"I will send you back," she says, careful not to let any irritation creep into her voice. "But first, you must tell me what your killer looks like."

Ruby huffs, "I don't know, bitch. He looked like a million other mediocre white dudes. Why do you want to know?"

"So that we can stop him."

Ruby is silent, for once. Then she asks, "Who is 'we'?"

Opal sighs. "That's a long story. Bear with me. I used to be a sex worker . . ."

"You mean you were a whore," Ruby says with venom in her voice. "No more of this PC 'woke' shit. You sucked dick for money."

Opal ignores Ruby's rudeness, though it's hard to do so. "I was a whore," she continues, "and I was good at it. Very good. And, because of my, let's call it, unique anatomy, I was very much in demand."

"You mean, you're a chick with a dick."

Opal cringes, but at first, refuses to rise to the bait. Then, anger gets the best of her. "I couldn't afford the surgery. It's not like I had a Cadillac insurance plan."

"I know that's right," Ruby says. Opal can't figure out if she's speaking in cynical solidarity or being sarcastic. She decides that it doesn't make a difference.

"One of my clients—johns—was a repeat customer. Let's call him Sam. Sam worked in international finance, and one time, he offered to take me with him to São Paolo. I'd never been out of the country, and I didn't know when I'd have the opportunity again, so I paid for an expedited passport and went with him.

"We were supposed to be there for the better part of a week, with an excursion to see Iguauzu Falls at the end. I had the time of my life, eating, drinking, and shopping like a princess. He had long meetings in the daytime, and I spent the time drinking caipirinhas like a fish and exploring the city. We stayed in a fabulous hotel, with a balcony room that overlooked the city. São Paolo goes on and on, as far as the eye can see. Tall buildings, bright lights everywhere you looked. It's like Manhattan multiplied! Little shantytowns, called favelas, are in the shadows of high-rises."

"It sounds *extra*," Ruby mutters.

Opal laughs. "It *is* extra. The population is something like 20 million, at least twice New York City's. It's also twice as busy. And twice as dangerous.

"Well, one night, Sam and I got into a fight. You see, he wanted to 'share' me with one of his colleagues. And the colleague was into some things that I don't do . . ."

"Bondage and domination?" Ruby asked.

"No, girl," Opal says. "I can handle whipping and yelling at white dudes. It was stuff like golden showers and strangling. Rough, dirty stuff I'm not comfortable doing. And I told Sam that, in no uncertain terms. Well, he offered to pay me more. I still refused. I'm not into piss play!"

"He wasn't respecting your limits," Ruby says.

"He called me an ungrateful bitch. Then said I could find my own accommodations."

"He kicked you out?" Ruby's shade flickered. "What a douchebag."

"A total fuckboy move. I left the fancy hotel with $100 dollars in Brazilian reals, my luggage, and my passport in a country where I didn't know the language. I was angry, and also scared to death. São Paolo isn't the safest place, mind you. I was a sex worker, but I had my pride. But somehow, by the grace of God, I found a place. It was a hostel, on the border of one of the favelas."

"So, a sketchy place."

"Yes. But you know what? It wasn't bad, for the first two nights. I was the only person there so I had the place to myself. I was in the women's section, in a room of bunk beds, and I had the shower all to myself. The desk clerk João was a real sweetheart. He couldn't have been more than 22. He had lovely olive-brownish skin, and the greenest eyes I have ever seen. He practiced his English with me, and told me a little about his life. He was from a small beach town in the north of the country, a place called Praia de Igaupe and moved to São Paolo because there were no jobs there. I could tell that he missed it. He told me that he had a sister who was 'a girl like me.' I was unsure of what he meant at the time.

"It all changed on the third night, when a group of German tourists took over the hostel. They were two men and two women. I was taking my afternoon shower after being out and about when one of the women passed by the shower stall and saw what she saw. Of course, Heidi or whatever her name was, freaked the fuck out, and she told her friends about me.

"That evening one of the males, let's call him Gunther, who could speak English well enough, told me I couldn't stay in the women's room, and made a big stink of it to João. João, bless his heart, was completely unfazed. He calmed those assholes down, and then told me that I could stay, at the same rate, in the empty apartment above the hostel. He told me that I was a child of Pomba Gira, whatever that meant, and I was lucky to have her favor. I thought it was an odd thing to say, and, mind you, his English wasn't the best and my Portuguese was non-existent at the time.

"The upstairs apartment was amazing, and not just because I had my own bathroom. It was tiny, with room for a twin-sized bed. The walls of the room were painted a beautiful ruby-red pomegranate color. The floor was tiled and wonderfully cool, given that the place wasn't air-conditioned. In a corner that might have been a tiny closet, there was an altar of some kind.

"There was a table covered with a cloth the same pomegranate color as the walls. In the center, there was the foot-high figurine of a red she-devil, naked as the day she was born, her tits out and proud, with a mischievous sneer on her face. She had horns, yes, but she was in no way demonic. In fact, she was cute. The figurine was surrounded by melted wax candles, along with an unopened pack of cigarettes and a half empty bottle of cachaça. At the time, I didn't understand the significance, and thought that the display was like the Brazilian equivalent of the Tiki gods. You know, some Pier One imports kind of shit.

"My last night in Brazil, I decided to go out. I mean, fuck Sam. Why the hell should I not have a good time? João told me about a good sushi place and gave me directions there. I managed to order the food without embarrassing myself, and even treated myself to some sake.

"Well, not some sake. I had two lychee-flavored saketinis along with a couple of shots."

"Go ahead, girl," Ruby says. Her form is more substantial now, looking less like a hologram.

"I got *turnt*, and got lost on the way back to the hostel. One street looked like another and before too long, I found myself stumbling into one of the favelas. There were no streetlights overhead, and the pavement was uneven. The buildings looked haphazardly put together, made out of corrugated tin, shipping containers, and cracking concrete. The only lights came from candles, kerosene lamps, or strung-up Christmas lights. Feral cats slunk about, and the narrow streets were empty.

"I wandered around, going down streets, hoping to find some place I recognized. But it was no use. I turned around one corner, and saw a group of four or five young men, around João's age. They were all huddled up, puffing weed cigarettes, whispering and laughing. One of them saw me. I moved away from them, but they could see that I was lost and afraid, so they surrounded me in a vaguely threatening manner.

"Of course, I couldn't understand them, but I could guess that what they were saying was lewd, because their voices were rowdy. They egged each other on, flashing grilles and gold teeth. One of them draped his arms across my shoulder in a painful grip.

"He began stroking my hair. The others closed in on me. And I knew that it was only a matter of moments before the assault began. I felt that mixture of helplessness and rage I'm sure you're familiar with."

Ruby nods her assent.

"I braced myself for the worst, a fight I would almost definitely lose.

"Then, we all heard it. The clop-clop-clop of high heels on uneven pavement. The gang fell silent. So did I, for some reason, even though it would be the perfect moment to yell for help. I think that I was surprised at the loudness of the sound. It was definitely a brazen gait.

"The footsteps stopped, and around the corner there came a woman. Though, the word 'woman' does not really do her justice. She wore stiletto heels that made her tower over everyone, which she would have done even if she hadn't worn them. The heels themselves were sharp and transparent, like icicles or glass shards. She could have easily slit a throat with them if she needed to. She wore a gown the color of pomegranates, an off-the-shoulder gown that glowed like a neon sign. Her hair was a storm cloud of black curls, rippling on an unfelt breeze. Her skin was soft brown, her lips luscious and dewy. She had large breasts that defied gravity. And her eyes—they were black. Blackety black. And ancient, like a piece of onyx yet to be mined.

"The woman took in the scene before her. Then, she threw back her head and *laughed*. Heartily, a throaty staccato chuckle. 'You boys are looking for trouble. But trouble has found *you*!'

"She spoke in Portuguese, but I could understand her—every word. The gang member who held me said something that was probably not nice, definitely crude.

"'You couldn't handle us with your tiny little worm-like cocks. I can smell your nasty crotch from here! What did you all do—wash them with shit?' she asked.

"Another gang member called her a long chain of something that probably included the c-word. And she, in her pomegranate glory, said, 'My vagina is sacred. Your diseased bird dicks would shrivel up inside. I am the Eater of little boys who think they are big men!'

"The man who had grasped me let me go, and lunged for the strange and apparently insane woman in the red dress. He grabbed her forearm, and he immediately jumped back as if he had been stung. His hand was red and smoking. She laughed that machine-gun laugh of hers, her head thrown back, laughing wildly.

"Another gang member spat at her. She fixed him with her cobra glare, and I saw the ring around her pupils turn red. The same color as the room I now stayed in. And I knew then, that she was the real version of the she-devil doll in the small alcove in my room. Her divinity rolled off her in invisible waves.

"'Leave both of us alone,' she shouted, 'leave at once! Or your dicks will be flaccid slugs for the rest of your miserable lives. Your balls will shrivel to the size of raisins, and your cum will stink of rotten fish!'

"The gang were inching away from her at this time. One of them flashed a switchblade.

"'Your little metal dick is worthless,' she said. And the blade flopped over, as if it had been melted. Then she began to dance, some variation on the samba that incorporated lots of twirls. She spun faster and faster, like a Whirling Dervish. The pomegranate fabric of her dress unspooled and got longer and longer until they became snakes, red cobras that struck out at the retreating gang."

"That's some crazy story," Ruby says. She now glows, in sharp definition. "I wish I'd had a guardian she-devil."

Opal wished that she could have touched Ruby, held her hand, comforted her. She said, "She has many names, but the followers of Quimbanda and Umbanda call her Pomba Gira. She's the patron saint of girls like us. She can't bring you back to life. But, she can avenge you. And save other sisters."

"So, she's the goddess of Ratchet Hos?"

Opal laughed. "In a manner of speaking. But she is so much more! We are her children."

Ruby's form shimmered, winking in and out of the liminal shadows. "I have one question," she said after a while. "Can she fuck him up?"

The Nectar of Nightmares

The nectar of nightmares is an acquired taste. It is impossible to catalog all of the flavor profiles. It can taste of bitter chocolate, old licorice, astringent gasoline, slightly turned meat, or rancid butter. Each batch of nectar is different, in texture and color. Some might be thick, sludgy, and syrupy, and another batch might a thin, salty broth.

Sweet, with acidic notes

The Swan Girl first came to Tori when she was ten years old.

At the time, she'd been taking ballet classes at the Petrochenkov Dance Studio. She was a star pupil, full of grace and flexibility. She could stretch her small body into any shape, and *glissé, pilé,* and grand *jeté* with ease. It was as if her bones were made of rubber. The various forms and poses of ballet were like a second, secret language made of movement. She loved it all: the music, the outfits, and most of all, the moment when the routine became effortless muscle memory.

Her instructor, Mademoiselle du Plessis, (also known as The Mad Lady) called her "my little Leda." The nickname sounded so intriguing.

"Who is Leda?" she asked the Mad Lady one time after class. The other students called her the Mad Lady, both because she was so harsh and the word "mademoiselle" was kind of hard to say. But Tori had a girl-crush on her. The Mad Lady looked like a living statue. You could see the fine architecture of her bones, so long and thin, beneath her olive skin and gauzy dresses. She had a high forehead and sunken eyes that gave her an alien quality.

"You know nothing of Leda and the Swan? Read your mythology," was all she said. The Mad Lady had no patience for the American education system, where everything was sanitized. So, Tori did read the myth of Leda, after being directed to the appropriate book by the kind school librarian. And she was promptly horrified. The story was about a woman who had sex with a swan, got pregnant by him, and laid a couple of eggs. There was no part of the story that wasn't disgusting. Even worse, there was a whole series of paintings of this improbable union, all of them featuring a naked lady with a swan nestled between her legs.

After one class, Tori told her that she'd read the myth, and still didn't understand why she'd earned the nickname Leda. "The woman laid *eggs*," Tori said, expecting her ballet instructor to be as repulsed as she had been.

Mme du Plessis had (illegally) lit a cigarette. Dirty blue smoke cascaded from her nostrils. She was clearly annoyed.

"You misunderstand, child," the Mad Lady finally said, "You have been blessed with the *grace* of a swan. You are the swan's child. Eggs have nothing to do with it."

She waved Tori's apparent stupidity away, along with the smoke.

"Oh," said Tori, though she really didn't understand at all. To her, the myth was borderline perverse. Did Leda even want to mate with a swan? Tori's grasp on bedroom activities was tenuous at best, but wouldn't sex with a swan be painful? Or even, possible? She forgot the nickname and the myth; it was just one more Grown-Up thing she didn't get. (And maybe Mme. du Plessis actually was a mad lady).

There the whole incident stayed buried until the recital. *Swan Lake* was a staple of ballet companies, a rite of passage, and the Petrochenkov School elected to perform an abbreviated version of the perennial classic. There were to be auditions, mostly to assuage anxious parents, but everyone knew that Tori would be cast as Odette, the Swan Queen. It was a given.

During the announcement of the recital, the Mad Lady said, "Ballet is not *just* about movement. A ballet is a story told through the medium of dance. It is vital that you understand the story behind *Swan Lake*. You Americans always tone things down."

She then told the plot of the the legend the ballet was based upon. It was a savage, tragic story, one that Tori didn't like at all. It was even *worse* than the Leda story.

That was the first night the Swan Girl visited her. In the dream, her curtains were open, and the moon was gigantic and took up most of the sky. Tori lay in her bed, facing the magnificent moon, which filled her room like a silver floodlight. Then, it cracked. The moon split in two with a horrible, jarring sound. Dream-Tori clapped her hands, thrilled at this turn of events. She loved it when dreams became weird, like cartoons. Once, she had had a long, sur-realistic adventure that featured Strawberry Shortcake, a couple of the Bratz dolls, and the cute guy from that Nickelodeon show.

Something emerged from the broken silver shell of the moon. A white arm, followed by another, stretched across the sky. The arms unfolded, and used two sparkling stars as leverage. The white arms pushed up, and a head emerged from the cracked moon. It was a woman with short, shockingly white hair. She had a beautiful face with delicate features. Her eyebrows were the same white color as the hair on her head. She smiled at Tori, from a million miles away. And in that smile, Tori saw her teeth.

Her teeth were terrible things. They weren't even teeth-shaped. They were sharp, glittering things, more like knives. And they were transparent, as if the woman who had hatched from the moon had a mouth full of broken glass. Tori saw that her white "hair" was really feathers—thousands of fluffy white feathers. Suddenly, she wasn't beautiful at all.

Tori thought, *At least she is far away.*

I am not far from you at all, said the Swan Girl. *I can travel faster than fast.* Then the Swan Girl ripped the remaining pieces of moon into smaller fragments then scattered them across the sky.

Tori woke up in a cold sweat. She got up, and looked out the window. The moon was just a sliver, and kind of yellow. There was no way it could be a giant egg-prison for that horrible woman. At ten, she was imminently reasonable. Her life was mapped out. She would have a brief, glorious career in dance, after which she would go to college and study something practical, like law or math. She would get married and have kids—hopefully one boy and one girl—and live in a nice, two-story rambler. She knew that the dream was just the result of nerves, or too much orange chiffon cake (she re-ally shouldn't have had that second piece, as small as it was), and the Mad Lady's collection of slightly inappropriate stories roaming around her head. (Did Mademoiselle du Plessis know any happy fairy-tales?) She went back to sleep without a second thought.

The nightmare left her mind as she delved into the next week's school and homework. Saturday rolled around, and with it, the auditions at the Petrochenkov Dance Studio. To the surprise of no-one, she landed the role of Odette. Since the class was all female, a couple of sturdier-built girls were cast as the evil wizard and the handsome prince. Dillon MacKenzie complained about being cast as the wizard; was it because she was black, and evil was always black? And Marjorie Kincaid, who was the prince, didn't want anyone thinking she was a lezzie. The Mad Lady told Dillon that she was "silly," and told Marjorie that she was portraying a prince; if she were playing a princess, then she would be a lesbian. And even then, she would just be *playing* a lesbian. Tori knew better than to ask Mme du Plessis what a lesbian was. She had a vague idea, anyway, and thought the Mad Lady might be one, herself.

It was a great day, by all accounts. Her mother was as pleased as punch to learn her daughter was so talented; she even teared up. So, Tori was surprised when the Swan Girl visited her again.

This time, Tori was on the moon itself. She didn't remember how she had gotten there. It was a cold, hollow, and desolate place, all monochromatic like an old black and white movie. Tori glanced up into the void of space, and saw the Swan Girl winging towards her. Her wings were wide and beautiful. They shimmered in the cold light of the stars. But the closer she got, the more Tori could see her gleaming glass teeth.

The Swan Girl gracefully landed on a grey and white lunar hillock, next to Tori. Tori noticed that she didn't have the webbed feet of a swan; her legs were stalks that ended in barbed claws.

The two regarded each other silently.

Then, Tori said, *If we're on the moon, how can I breathe?*

The Swan Girl seemed to consider this. She said, *Perhaps you aren't alive. Maybe I've taken your soul, and your body lays as dead as a dormouse in your snug little bed.* Then she grinned. A cave of glass knives flashed.

"This is getting ridiculous," Tori said aloud, when she woke up.

Rehearsals started immediately, along with set design, and costume fittings. Rehearsals took place both on Wednesdays after school and Saturday mornings. Each session was a grueling two hours, and Tori found that her body began to ache. The bones of her feet began to throb. She began to understand what Aunt Mariska meant when she would talk about her "barking dogs." Though, to Tori, her feet weren't just barking; they felt as if they'd been attacked by a pack of rabid dogs. She began wrapping and icing her feet. The Mad Lady became even harsher, threatening to cancel the recital at the smallest mistake or imperfection. "I will not be embarrassed by you," she said. In fact, it became her catch-phrase. Tori lost her girl-crush on Mme du Plessis. The frown on her long face made her look grotesque, and her thinness reminded Tori of those super creepy Picasso sculptures she once saw at the museum. She began to hate ballet. It was torture.

The night after every rehearsal, the Swan Girl came to visit her. The venues were varied. One time, Tori was alone in the rehearsal space when the Swan Girl appeared in one of the mirrors. The creature began stretching, using the reversed balance bar. Then she danced. She was terrible. Despite her swanhood, she was graceless and clunky, and her wings got in the way. She laughed as she mimicked the movements of Odette, and Tori found herself laughing along, until the Swan Girl flashed her diamond-hard teeth. Another time, Tori was stranded on a boulder in the middle of a lake the color of a blue raspberry slushie when the Swan Girl landed on the lake's shore. She was carrying a large handbag, an expensive one made of brown leather and embossed with a gold maze-like shape. The Swan Girl waved at Tori, and opened the bag, producing the softly rotting head of Mme. du Plessis. Fruit flies hovered around the head, and jeweled the bright red viscera dripping from her neck. The Swan Girl hurled the severed head to Tori. And the severed head, in mid-flight, opened its mouth and screamed.

Tori told no one about the Swan Girl. What was there to tell? She suspected that the Swan Girl was stress-induced, but she was unwilling to give up ballet even though she currently hated it. Ballet was something she was good at. It was a part of her— maybe the best part. The Swan Girl was something she had to endure. She would tell her parents about the creature only after the recital. She hoped that there would be no need to, though. Not if the Swan Girl was a manifestation of some deep-seated fear.

Gradually, the troupe got better and better. Best of all, Tori's muscle memory took over. Now she leapt, glided, balanced, pirouetted without thought. She was pure movement. The score and the plot were merely guidelines. The Swan Girl visited her one night, emerging from the show's poster, a reproduction of an old lithograph that showed a swan in flight. In the dream, Tori was performing with the troupe. The Swan Girl hovered above it all and began shooting her cast-mates with arrows made of pinions of her feathers. She shot Dillon in the throat, and Marjorie in the heart. Both bled profusely, rivers of blood making the floor slick. More arrows, more deaths. Kenya Smyth, Jade Arthur, Yvonne Tallis, all with vacant stares, sightlessly watching Tori as she danced her heart out. She danced perfectly.

The evening of the first performance came. The night before had been dreamless, and she moved through the hours of the day in a trance. Mom, Dad, Aunt Mariska, and even her sister Antoinette were supportive and encouraging. *You've worked so hard,* one of them said. *You'll be great,* said another. *We love you so much,* said someone. *You'll become my sister,* said someone.

"What are you talking about?" snapped Tori. "You are my sister, dweeb."

"Huh?" Ant looked genuinely confused. Ant was a brat, but maybe she hadn't spoken. Then who had?

She and her family went in separate directions: they to the audience, she backstage. Tori was numb as she dressed herself and her makeup was applied. She was filled with dread. She rationalized it as routine stage fright, pre-performance jitters. But somehow, she knew that it was something more.

You'll become my sister.

Now, she looked like a swan maiden. White tulle, silver embroidery. A tiara of rhinestones. She even had a little shawl of gauzy white material: her "wings." She was so beautiful, she could dance with her sister—not Ant—her *true* sister forever.

"Ladies!" Mme. du Plessis's grating voice demanded order. Girls stopped running hither and yon, stood still, as if playing the game Stop Light. Instead of an inspirational speech, the instructor told them all not to embarrass her, or themselves. Oh, how she hated the Mad Lady, with her sadistic know-it-all attitude. Someone—her true sister—should slice off her head, shut her right up.

Tori heard Tchaikovsky on the piano, so distant and tiny. The show was about to begin. Tori walked to the stage on her pit bull-mauled feet. The lake was made of shimmery blue fabric, and the lights in shades of emerald and honey bathed the stage. She and the other swan maidens entered, on their toes. And promptly, Tori forgot where she was, maybe even who she was. The world shrank, became only sound and movement.

Her feet no longer hurt. She no longer felt anything, only a sense of *rightness* when her body made the correct form. There was no floor, no stage, no audience. Just her, tumbling through— through what? Her eyes were open, but they did not see.

And suddenly, she *did* see.

The world was empty. There was a stage, illuminated by smears of emerald and honey light, and there were seats, all velvety black. But she was alone in the world. No other dancers. No Mad Lady. No mother, father, aunt or sister. Just her, and—

It glowed, somewhere in the center of the theater. It was a layered glow, opaque white and translucence mingled together. What was it that glowed?

The Swan Girl ascended from her seat, like an angel. Her arms were open wide, waiting for Tori to fly into them. Her glass teeth sparkled like diamonds.

Sister.

A strange taste rose in her mouth. It was sweet, yet it burned her palate.

Salt, with a floral undertone

"Come on," said Silvia, "don't be such a chickenshit."

Connie loved it when Silvia cursed. It was sexy. It was badass. Silvia had a great voice, all gravel, menthol cigarettes, and hard liquor. When she cursed, the harsh consonants were verbal gun-fire, and they made Connie all moist. Not that she'd ever tell Silvia that she had a crush on her. Still, Connie eyed the flask suspiciously. It had a silver mustang embossed on the front, galloping through a burlap landscape. Too many people she knew ended up in some psych ward or rehab because they drank or smoked some illicit substance or another. She could count them off on her fingers. Jimmy. Elaine. Verne. Jody. Would she be the fifth one?

Silvia swigged some of the stuff she called Purple Drank and passed it to her. It was sunset, spectacular on its own without any chemical enhancement. The sun had just gone behind some cliffs, and a sliver of moon floated in a sky the color of blue raspberry slushies. The horizon was green, pink and orange. They both lay in the bed of Silvia's pickup, looking up at the emerging stars.

Or, at least Connie was looking at the sky. Silvia was already nodding off, caught in the spell of the Purple Drank. Damn, she looked so fucking hot, lightly sheened with sweat, her cute little breasts rising up and down on her chest as she breathed. Maybe something would happen between them, if she drank the stuff. What harm could it do, just one time?

Silvia's dad worked for a drugstore pharmacy, so getting the medicated cough syrup wasn't a big deal.

"He gets samples all the time. We have Vicodin, Oyxies— Percocet's all over the place."

(Connie didn't know what those drugs were, so she just nodded as if she were impressed).

Silvia had found a recipe for Purple Drank on one of the online hip-hop forums she frequented.

Connie sipped it cautiously. It tasted good, kind of like grape soda. Not the natural stuff, but the supermarket brand, sweet and fizzy and somehow *purple*-tasting. She drank more, and in a few minutes, began feeling all warm and silly. The feeling crept up from the pit of her belly, up her spine and nestled in the center of her brain. She wanted to sleep and she wanted to stay awake forever. It was like how you felt when you stayed up too late and got a little loopy and the whole world was just full of jokes that made you laugh. You giggled until you burst. Every cell inside of her began to giggle like a thirteen-year-old girl.

A tremor of joy travelled through her nerves. She opened her eyes, to see what Silvia was doing.

Instead, she saw a naked boy sitting on a rock formation, looking at the truck's flatbed. She was speechless. None of it made any sense. His nudity, for one thing. Then, there was the thing with his hair. It was dust colored, not exactly grey or white. And he had a lot of it, on his head, chest, and yes, his groin. A thick shelf of it formed a unibrow. His face was ugly, almost f(ucking)-ugly. A nose that was grotesquely upturned, eyes too big and a sickly shade of blue, bizarrely large ears furred with even more dusty hair. Connie saw his junk was erect. It was an ugly thing, an orangey-red rod. And his nails were long and filthy. But the worst thing of all were his teeth. They were jagged and uneven. And they had a weird shine to them.

I like to watch, he said. *Make your move, already!*

At first, Connie wanted to curse him out, chase him away with *Shut up, you limp-dicked perv.* Then she noticed that he didn't actually speak in a physical sense. His mouth, with its weird glass teeth, didn't move at all. Somehow, his words, and the sound of his voice, just formed in her head.

"You're just a hallucination," she said. Silvia stirred with a "huh?"

That's what you think. You'll see, he replied. He scratched his balls. Then he leapt up off the rock formation and ran away in an awkward-looking skitter-crawl, kicking up a cloud of dust.

It was an odd incident, but since she was a virgin to illicit substances, she assumed that hallucinations were normal. When she mentioned the Grey Boy to Silvia, she found out just how weird it was.

"You sure you saw a naked boy?" said Silvia afterwards. "I've never seen anything like that on Purple Drank. It just makes me feel real chill. I only ever saw stuff on shrooms."

Connie made a note to herself to never to try shrooms. The Grey Boy wasn't exactly scary, but the idea of a dream figure that spoke to her was deeply uncomfortable. She knew that everyone reacted differently to drugs. She, for instance, always became super sleepy on Sudafed even though it made everyone else hyper. Maybe it was because of this, but Connie stopped hanging around Silvia, which turned out to be a good thing, since a few weeks later Silvia was sent to jail for beating up another girl.

But Connie had a thing for bad girls. She couldn't help it; maybe it was in her DNA. Dad's girlfriends all had prison records or stints in psychiatric hospitals. He always told her, "I guess I like a challenge," after the relationships crashed and burned. Maybe she liked challenges, too. And Ray was a challenge.

For starters, Ray was older than Connie—maybe in her early 20s. It wasn't clear. Another thing that wasn't clear was her gender. She had short hair and wore men's clothing—rolled up jeans, leather vests, and bolo ties. Her hair was done up in a pompadour style, like the pictures of young Elvis. Her arms were covered with all kinds of tattoos. Wiley E. Coyote, beautiful skull-faced girls with marigolds wound through their hair, a couple of phrases in Diné Bizaad. She didn't get mad when people called her "sir," and it was rumored that if you called her by her birth name, she would punch your lights out. All of these made Ray hella sexy.

A thing that was problematic: she sold drugs. Connie tried staying away from drugs, but bad girls and drugs went together. They were a fatal combination. So here she was, sitting in Ray's trailer, decorated with Navajo textiles and sugar skulls, about to take "Molly." Connie wasn't really sure what "Molly" was supposed to do. She knew it was a party drug, done at raves and clubs. So why were they doing it here, alone, in Ray's trailer?

Ray began streaming music from her computer, something with disembodied vocals and hypnotic melodic patterns. She handed Connie a pill that had an eye embossed on it from a bottle, and took one for herself.

"Remember to drink lots of water," said Ray. And she took hers.

Before she could back out, Connie took hers.

"Come on," said Ray after a moment, "let's take a walk."

Both of them left the trailer, after Ray tossed a bottle of water to Connie and took one herself. Ray's trailer was at the edge of the mobile community. It was called *The Desert Rose*, but half of the trailers were empty, so Ray called it *The Deserted Rose*. They wandered away from the highway and into the desert proper. Agave bushes, stunted cactus plants, and witchy-looking Joshua trees dotted the landscape. The sky was purple-black, and the moon was full. It was gorgeous. All at once, Connie fell in love with world. Earlier in the week she'd complained about where she lived, always so dry and dusty. She used the word "wasteland" because it was featureless and grey and beige. Dust and sand seemed to cover everything, a permanent grime that it was futile to get off cars, furniture or skin. But now, illumined by moonlight and starlight, she saw the fierce beauty of the land. Her heart swelled with it. Every grain of sand was suddenly sacred. She heard the howl of a lone coyote and she loved that coyote as if it were a beloved pet. She could imagine its head thrown back in an almost religious ecstasy, singing to the moon.

"I love this place!" Connie shouted. She couldn't contain her love. She wanted to howl, too, like her brother, the coyote.

"Dude," said Ray, "chill." She flashed her pearly whites at Connie. "You're really rolling."

Connie caught up with her, and took her hand. She could feel Ray's pulse. Ray squeezed her hand back.

Molly was a million times better than Purple Drank. Connie had never felt so happy in her entire life. She glanced up at the stars, and fell in love again. The stars weren't just white. They were tinged with colors like violet and crimson. There were so many of them! She felt another howl lodged in her throat, threatening to erupt.

Before she could howl to the moon, there was some rustling in the creosote bush. Ray jumped back, and gave an uncharacteristically girly scream. She gripped Connie's hand tightly. Tough-as-nails Ray was scared, and Connie, in her lace-edged dress and wedges, was not. After all, what could it be? A rabbit, or maybe a lone javelina. Something that was probably just hiding from them.

"Dude, chill," said Connie.

Ray laughed, flashing those perfect teeth of hers. She still eyed the bush warily. And the bush shivered again. And Ray ran, hauling ass.

"Ray, it's nothing. Probably just an itty-bitty bunny rabbit." But Ray was already maybe fifteen feet away.

A sober Connie probably would have followed her. But Connie, on Molly, was reckless and adventurous. She made soothing clicks with her voice, towards the creosote bush, which was starred with yellow flowers. And from behind the bush emerged—

The Grey Boy. He was as nude, as hairy and as erect as she'd remembered him from a year ago. Connie didn't know if she should scream, or laugh. She turned around, and saw Ray running away, at full throttle speed. Ray wasn't so tough, after all.

Some winner you got there, the Grey Boy said.

"Fuck you," said Connie. Then she laughed. It was ridiculous, all of it. This apparition. Her experiments with mind-altering substances. Her attraction to bad women. "Fuck it all," she said aloud.

Maybe it was the Molly coursing through her brain, but suddenly everything was crystal-clear. Her path in life, her mistakes, and how to correct them.

The Grey Boy grinned at her, an almost doglike grin. His glass teeth reflected the cold light of the stars.

Connie's fear rose in her gorge. Fear tasted of salt, and, faintly, dead flowers.

Bitter, with a metallic aftertaste

It came to Lionel this time in the guise of his mother, in her younger years. In her 30s, Imogene Greaves was a looker. All of his male friends had a crush on her. And here she was, dolled-up in a brown paisley miniskirt that barely covered her ass, white platform boots, and a fluffy, mile-high Afro. She even wore those large, goggle-like sunglasses. She could have been a Black Panther, or at least a member of the Mod Squad. This was the Imogene who grooved to the 5th Dimension and Earth, Wind & Fire, smoked Virginia Slims and could quote Gwendolyn Brooks and Langston Hughes by heart. This was not the older Imogene, a husk of a woman who battled prescription pain addiction and was meaner than Idi Amin, Baby Jane, and Mike Tyson combined. Still, Lionel knew it was a trick. For one thing, his mother was long dead, by at least a decade. He wasn't even sure they made clothes like that anymore. And where his mother met him was all wrong. It was at the empty mess hall from his time in Iraq. There was no way she had never been overseas, let alone, Iraq.

"What the hell you want," Lionel said.

It didn't answer. It never did. Instead, his mother opened her mouth, revealing those awful transparent spikes that were her teeth, and beckoned him, opening her arms.

"Fuck you," he said, "leave me the hell alone!"

Some of her hair fell off. An earring, then an ear. Right on the mess hall floor. Still, she invited him to hug her—

"Sir, wake up!"

This command was followed by three sharp raps.

"Sir." The voice sounded annoyed.

Lionel opened his eyes reluctantly. How long had he been out? Not long enough. He felt the symphony of aches and pains begin.

He blinked into focus. A uniformed man was staring down at him. He sat at a table strewn with books and magazines. Then he remembered that he was at the library.

"There's no sleeping here." The security guard glared at him, a warning. "If you nod off again, I'm going to have to ask you to leave."

Lionel said, "Okay," and began rifling through the nearest magazine. Cosmo, that featured some white female celebrity he didn't recognize on the cover. He flipped through the magazine, resting his eyes on a list-style article about spicing up your sex-life.

He was pathetic. The way his life was now. He forced himself not to think about odd numbers.

Libraries used to be awesome places, temples full of scholars and bookworms devouring the written word in reverent silence. Not now. Computers had replaced the books, and cellphones vibrated, and occasionally rang, interrupting the silence. And instead of scholars, there were homeless people seeking refuge from the heat.

Homeless people like himself.

He put the magazine aside. If he was going to stay awake, he might as well be useful.

He approached the information desk, acutely self-aware of his filthy, disheveled appearance. He probably smelled as well, but he was used to his own stink. Still, he was a goddamned human being. The librarian behind the desk was a white dude with shoulder-length hair and large, Clark Kent-like glasses. Lionel cleared his throat, politely.

The librarian looked up from his computer screen.

"Where are the books on nightmares?" he asked.

"Excuse me?"

"Books on nightmares. Dreams."

"One moment," said the librarian. He began typing something into his search engine. He pulled out a piece of scrap paper, and wrote some a long number on it. He gave Lionel directions: third floor, in Psychology.

The first two books he found were too academic. They referred to various complexes and cognitive processes. The third book, however, was exactly what he was looking for. It had a catchy title: *A Herd of Nightmares*. But what really convinced Lionel was the cover of the book. It was a detail of a painting that featured a woman in a long white dress asleep on an ornate four-poster bed. A small demonic man crouched on her belly, grinning evilly. A horse's head leered on at this grotesque scene.

Lionel felt immediate recognition. It took on many shapes. His dead mother. His ex-wife. A schoolyard bully, his commanding lieutenant. The small, dark dwarf, and, perhaps, the horse itself, was one Its many forms. The only thing missing from the painting were the glass teeth.

The text of the book was a little over Lionel's head, but one chapter, on Lucid Dreaming, caught his attention. It was full of tips for confronting, and ultimately, changing the course of a dream. He wished that he could take notes. There were some good tips there.

The shelter was up to capacity that evening, so Lionel went to his old standby: downtown, in the enclosed area outside a department store, near a subway entrance. He was not alone. At least four other people squatted there for the night in their cocoons of makeshift bedding. Men and at least one woman nested in sleeping bags, rubber foam, industrial grey blankets—scant protection from the hard concrete. None of them spoke to each other, which was just fine. You never knew who you'd met. Junkies were the worst; they'd start fights with you. He'd been stabbed once by one in the throes of a drug-induced psychosis. He knew that sleep would be difficult. He could never really rest when he was out on the street.

Surprisingly, he found it easy to drift to unconsciousness. It was probably because he'd had such poor rest before. Lionel found himself in the storefront church where his uncle Vaughn used to preach. The church was called Clinic for the Hurt, and it was located in an old laundromat. You could still see the places where the washers and dryers had been, rust marks on worn linoleum tiles. The large windows were covered with a rough mosaic of tinted cellophane in various colors. The effect drenched the shabby interior (which was basically all made up of rows of folding chairs) in stained glass colors. As if it were a real church. There was a platform made of cinderblock where Uncle Vaughn would preach from. "Preach," though, an imprecise word. It was more like he hollered Scripture with his bullfrog-deep voice. His flock would go into ecstatic paroxysms, and Vaughn would smite them with his righteous anger. Minor aches and pains would subside, briefly. Lionel was skeptical at best, but to his credit, his uncle never claimed that he could heal anyone.

The Clinic for the Hurt was empty, and bathed in late afternoon light. It looked much better than it had in Real Life. For instance, the cellophane windows were *actually* stained glass. A triptych tableaux spread out on the glass. The first part showed a lake made of milky-blue glass out of which rose a woman garbed in a white, feathery garment. She had the wings of a swan on her back, but Lionel didn't think this thing was beautiful. It was somewhat sinister. Maybe it was the grin the piece depicted, with a flash of sharp teeth. The middle part of the triptych showed a desert scene in beige-yellows and tan browns. Behind an olive-green cactus, a half-nude boy peeked. The boy was grey as dust, skin, hair, and eyes. The only part of him that wasn't grey were the white serrated edges of his teeth, frozen in a grin. The third and final part showed a brown-skinned man who stood on platform made of cinderblocks. Like the other figures, it flashed its teeth.

The final figure of glass moved. One moment, it was animated glass, and in the next, Uncle Vaughn stepped from window.

Lionel knew what to do. He spun around three times. The book had told him that this technique would allow him to get control of the dream. The third and final spin. The world cracked. Fragmented, shattered. The Clinic for the Hurt fell away, in glittering shards. Even Uncle Vaughn broke apart. Skin, glass; it was impossible to determine what substance it was made of.

When the world lay in pieces on the ground, Lionel found himself quite alone. Where was he? The place where he stood was unfinished, and spare. The predominant color was beige—the same color as the mess hall in Iraq. In a far corner, a crystal blue lake gleamed, and swans silently patrolled its waters. In another corner, sand and weird, grey-green shrubs sprouted from the ground. A lone coyote with a dust-colored coat stalked the shrubs, its red tongue lolling out. And Lionel knew that he wasn't alone.

"Show yourself," he said. Or, at least, he thought he said that. The sounds stretched out so thin that they disappeared into the still air of the dream arena. But it must have had an effect because Lionel sensed a change in the air. The two vistas—the desert and the lake—faded away. And the mess hall became even more indistinct. And—the air seemed to thicken with a kind of humid density without the heat or wetness.

Then suddenly, *It* was there.

Palette Cleansing

It was in the shape of a human. It had both breasts and a penis. But it had no eyes, or ears, and the flesh was made of some reflective stuff. Lionel saw his face mirrored in its body, distorted to funhouse shapes.

The room had changed again. There was no mess hall, desert or lake. There was no landscape; he could have been in a room in a warehouse, save there were no windows.

Two other people were with him in the space. One was a white girl of ten or eleven— she wore a leotard, and her hair was pulled back into a tight little bun. The other was a young woman, maybe eighteen or twenty. He couldn't determine her ethnicity—she could have been Filipino or Latina with her rich reddish-brown skin, and her hair, which was in a short bob with forehead-obscuring bangs, was straight and pure black, save for one candy-red streak. The girl looked frightened. She was shivering and looked on the verge of tears. The woman looked pissed; she had murder in her eyes.

(Please, don't be afraid). The words just appeared in his head. The little girl began to cry. The young woman began muttering curse words under her breath.

(I mean no harm. You have something I need. You nourish me).

"I don't want to be here," said the child.

The young woman swore at it.

Lionel said, "What do you want? Why are you bothering us?"

The answer appeared in each of their minds, and on the reflecting skin in vivid images.

It was born without context, and without form. It was just a consciousness, free of flesh. It roamed, drifting like a cloud for unmeasured moments. A century, a millennium, or a minute. None of these had any meaning. Then:

It heard. It saw. It felt. And, most importantly, it tasted. Dream and hallucination (waking dreams) spilled and scented the world. Distilled, they produced a nectar, full of emotion and images that were succulent and nourishing. It devoured this nectar for a time, indiscriminately until it began craving certain kinds of flavors.

"So, we're your fucking private reserve," said the young woman.

(I mean you no harm!)
The young girl said, "I stopped dancing because of you."

Lionel said, "You're a parasite." He turned to the woman and the girl. "You can fight this. You can take control."

It turned into his grandmother, with her silver-grey hair and fringed shawl wrapped against its body.

"No," said Lionel. And the shawl constricted about its body, strangling it. And his grandmother disappeared, replaced by the mirrored personage. It grew white wings. The girl said, "No," and the wings snapped off. Finally, it sprouted wolfish silver-grey hair all over its body, and its penis became painfully erect. The young woman didn't say no; she let loose a string of expletive. (The young girl covered her ears and eyes). The reflecting penis broke off—

Lionel sat up. It took a moment to regain his bearings—outside a subway station. He was sweating and cold as well.

Did it work?

However, he knew, with dread certainly, that *It* was not dead.

The dreamscapes it curated and so carefully developed were gone. It was time to move on to new minds, and new shapes.

Publication History

"Beneath the Briar Patch" (*Anathema*, August 2017)

"Myth and Moor" (*Evil in Technicolor*, Vernacular Press, 2020)

"Fur and Gold" (previously self-published)

"Black-Winged Roses" (*Revelator*, 2019)

"Underglaze" (*Nowhereville*, Broken Eye Books, 2019)

"Mirror Bias" (*Looming Low*, Dim Shores 2016)

"Eidolon Realty, LLC." (*Walk on the Weird Side*, NecromoniCon, 2017)

"(K)naivety" (*Forbidden Futures #7*, 2020)

"Sigilance" (previously unpublished)

"The Magus Club" (*Madder Love: Queer Men and the Precincts of Surrealism*, Rebel Satori Press, 2008)

"Spyder Threads" (*Come Join Us by the Fire*, Tor Nightfire, 2020)

"Desiccant" (*Slay: Stories of the Vampire Noire*, Mocha Memoirs Press, 2020)

"Sacred She-Devil" (*Whether Change: The Revolution Will be Weird*, Broken Eye Books, 2020)

"The Nectar of Nightmares" (Dim Shores, 2015).

About the Author

Craig Laurance Gidney is the author of *Sea, Swallow Me & Other Stories* (2008), *Bereft* (2013), *Skin Deep Magic: Short Fiction* (2014), and *A Spectral Hue* (2019).

He is a three-time Lambda Literary Award finalist; winner of a Bronze Moonbeam and a Silver IPPY Award; and a Carl Brandon Parallax Award finalist. He lives in his native Washington, D.C.

Printed in Great Britain
by Amazon